D0350909

WARRIORS OF THE
BLACK SHROUD

PETER HOWE

HARPER

An Imprint of HarperCollins*Publishers*

Library of Congress Cataloging-in-Publication Data
Howe, Peter.
Warriors of the black shroud / by Peter Howe. — 1st ed.
p.   cm.
Summary: A shy, bookish boy is pulled into an underground
land called Nebula and asked to lead a kingdom in its fight against
darkness.
ISBN 978-0-06-172987-4
[1. Fantasy.]   I. Title.
PZ7.H8377War   2012   2011026147
[Fic]—dc23   CIP
                                                                AC

Typography by Erin Fitzsimmons
11 12 13 14 15 LP/RRDH 10 9 8 7 6 5 4 3 2 1
❖
First Edition

*This book is dedicated
to the memory of
Max Lowry,
whose smile could banish darkness.*

CHAPTER 1

Walker felt himself tumbling through blackness. He knew Eddie was ahead of him, but he couldn't tell where. The darkness was deeper and more frightening than any he had ever experienced. He didn't know where he was going or what was happening. Sometimes he felt a floor beneath his feet, and then it vanished and he was floating like a lost space explorer. What if he drifted like this forever? He tried not to panic, but it was hard.

Suddenly his feet hit solid ground with a thud. He

swayed, trying to regain his balance, and looked around to get his bearings. Then he rubbed his eyes and stared again to make sure that what he saw wasn't some weird dream. He had landed in an ancient-looking city completely surrounded by high walls. Simple, low-roofed houses lined the wide avenue where he was standing. Only one building was bigger than the rest. It looked like a castle, and from its highest turret flew a flag that bore a sunlike symbol.

The sky above his head was the same inky blackness through which he had just fallen, but down here everything dazzled with light. In front of him a group of people watched a juggler keep a stream of balls flying from his hands in an arc above his head. Each ball glowed like a tiny planet, and so did the juggler and his audience. Everything was alive with light—the people, the buildings, even the flowers that edged the lawns in front of every house sparkled in their beds.

In the dark sky dozens of silver birds wheeled and soared, their broad wings catching the same wind currents that moved the flag. Their feathers were mirrored, and they glittered against the blackness. A young boy was walking down the street leading a baby dragon on a leash. It hopped along beside him, and every so often it would let out a huge plume, not of fire but a cloud of bright light. Then Walker heard the sound of hooves and turned to see a pure white horse with a long, wavy mane and a tail that almost touched the ground. Mounted on its back was a man dressed in armor that was mirrored like the birds' wings. In one hand he held a long, shiny lance, on top of which fluttered a pennant with the same emblem as the flag. The man bowed to Walker.

"Greetings, my lord," he said. "You are most welcome to Nebula."

This wasn't the usual way grown-ups spoke to Walker, but it didn't matter because he wasn't really listening. His whole concentration was focused on a spot midway between the horse's eyes. Protruding out of the center of the animal's forehead was a single short horn.

"Yes," said a familiar voice behind him, "it is what you think it is. They always get it wrong in books. They make the horn much too long. The poor creature's head would tip forward if it were any bigger. But then, they often get things wrong in books, I've found."

Walker whirled around to see Eddie leaning on his long, fearsome sword. Eddie also shone with a brilliant light, and the *B* on the Boston Red Sox jacket he always wore gleamed like a neon sign.

"Eddie!" Walker cried. "Everything is glowing, even you!"

"Of course!" said Eddie. "We all do here. Without light we would suffer a fate worse than a thousand deaths. You're glowing yourself, as a matter of fact."

Walker glanced down and, sure enough, all his clothing and every part of his skin radiated a soft light. He lifted one hand in front of his eyes, turning it as if it wasn't part of his body at all. It was strange, but also kind of wonderful.

"That's the way things are in Nebula," Eddie went on. "There are no days here, and no nights, either. This is how it is all the time. We live in light but we don't forget that the dark is always present just the other side of the city walls, and it could take over at any moment. That's why you're here. You have an appointment to see the king. We must hurry. He's waited long enough to meet you."

CHAPTER 2

Walker had first seen Eddie one day while reading in his favorite place, inside a large cardboard box that had recently held the family's new refrigerator. He had jammed the container into the gap between the woodpile and the stone wall in the large yard at the back of the old farmhouse where he lived with his parents. Walker loved the box. He liked the smell of the cardboard and the soft orange light that filtered in. It seemed safe and secure to him, but even more important, it felt private and his alone.

Therefore he was both surprised and more than a little irritated when his reading was interrupted by the sudden appearance of a strangely dressed boy about his own age. Walker didn't hear him approach, which was not surprising. He often got so immersed in a book that the outside world seemed to vanish. The boy had to crouch down to peer inside the box, using a long sword to balance himself. The weapon was broad, with a golden handle into which had been worked emblems that looked like the sun. He also carried an evil-looking dagger with the same markings in his waistband. Apart from these weapons the boy looked the same as most of the boys in Walker's neighborhood. He wore jeans and a T-shirt with a Boston Red Sox jacket that he had draped over his shoulders. But unlike the other boys Walker knew, he had shoulder-length red hair, on top of which he wore a fedora with a feather. But his most striking feature was his eyes. They were bright green, and shone eerily like two small flashlights.

"What are you reading history for?" he asked Walker, looking at the book that lay open on his knees. "History's bunk. Do you not know that? It's written by people who weren't there and have no idea what happened."

Walker didn't quite know how to respond to this,

which didn't matter because he didn't get the chance.

"All books are bunk, in my opinion," the boy continued, barely pausing for breath. "They're for people who'd rather think than take action. Action, my friend, is the secret of success in this life, not book learning. You can quote me on that."

"And who would I be quoting if I wanted to?" Walker asked.

"My name is Eddie," the boy replied. "Actually, it's Prince Edward the Soon-to-Be-Terrible if you want it in full."

"Yeah, right," snorted Walker. "A prince, huh? I didn't know royalty supported the Red Sox. Well, your royal princeness, why are you trespassing in my backyard?"

"Highness," Eddie corrected him, but ignored the question. "The proper term is 'highness,' although it's of no consequence where you're concerned. Anyone with the mark outranks me anyway."

"What mark?" asked Walker warily.

"That mark," Eddie said, leaning forward and pointing at Walker's face. "The mark of the Chosen."

Walker had a strange, star-shaped birthmark on his cheek. It had appeared on his face shortly after he was born. He had always hated it and now he covered it with his hand and turned his head away from Eddie's stare.

"I can't help having it," he said, "and if you don't like it you can leave this box, which is what I'd like you to do anyway."

"Of course you can't help it," agreed Eddie. "You're one of the lucky ones, born to good fortune."

When others made fun of his birthmark Walker usually dealt with it by just walking away. He would have left now, had Eddie not been blocking the only exit. But when he looked into Eddie's eyes he realized the boy was perfectly serious.

"But it's ugly," he protested. "How can that possibly be good fortune?"

"Where I come from," Eddie explained, "it means you're royalty, and speaking personally I've always thought it was remarkably fortunate to be royal—although it does have its downsides, of course, like everything else," he admitted.

"Where *do* you come from?" asked Walker.

"I come from time immemorial, and from no time at all. I come from the mists of Scotland, and the sun-baked plains of Africa. I have fought the English at

Bannockburn and the Confederate Army at Manassas—twice, as it happens. I am the spirit of the—"

"Yeah, yeah, yeah," interrupted Walker with an irritated sigh. "I mean, where did you just come from?"

"Oh," said Eddie. "Just come from—that would be the Kingdom of Nebula."

"Nebula?" Walker asked. "Where on earth is the Kingdom of Nebula?"

"Well, it's not actually on Earth," Eddie replied mysteriously. "It's more like it's in Earth. You'd have to go there to understand why there's no place like it. I'll show it to you if you like."

"No thanks," said Walker. This kid seemed crazy, and he was armed! Walker had to think of some way to get rid of him before he did something dangerous.

"No, I'm serious," Eddie assured him. "I could take you there. It'd be more fun than reading a book in a box, that I can guarantee."

Walker decided to humor him in the hope that he would go away.

"I can't go now," he replied. "I have my homework to do, and this book's due back at the library tomorrow, and I want to finish it."

"Homework!" Eddie exploded. "Library! I'm offering

to show you a place that's so amazing you'll be blown away, and you'd prefer to do your homework! Come with me—you'll never regret it, trust me."

"It's not that I don't trust you," Walker said. "It's that I don't believe you."

"Pshaw!" exclaimed Eddie.

Suddenly there was a thump on the top of the box, followed by two more in quick succession. Eddie peered cautiously over it, his hand on the hilt of his dagger.

"Walker Watson," came the sound of a jeering voice. "What's on your face?"

"Hey, wimpy Walker!" cried another. "Don't hit me with one of your books! If you do I'll tell your ma!"

"Who's that?" demanded Eddie.

"It's just the boys from down the road," Walker replied. "Their dad works for the farmer, Mr. Trumbell. Don't worry about them. They'll go away."

"Oh, they'll go away, all right," growled Eddie. "You'd better believe that."

He leaped up and headed toward the picket fence that ran in front of Walker's house.

"No!" yelled Walker. "Leave them alone, please!"

But it was too late. Walker stuck his head around the corner of the box to see Eddie going full tilt toward the four boys on the other side of the fence. He slashed at the air with his sword and made stabbing motions with the dagger in his other hand. His hat toppled from his head, releasing a mane of red hair that streamed behind him as he gathered speed.

"Run, you cowards, run!" he yelled.

The four boys on the other side of the fence were big and strong and a little older than Walker. They loved to fight and normally they would have stood their ground, but when they saw this wild boy they fled down the road, bumping into one another in their haste to get away. Eddie returned to the box grinning.

"There, that's the way to treat people like that," he said. "Remember, my friend, a bully is either at your throat or at your feet, and I know which one I prefer."

"I wish you hadn't done that," sighed Walker. "Now they'll tell their dad and he'll come and complain to my dad, and how I'm going to explain you I have no idea. And that Daniel, the biggest one—he's mean. He won't forget this quickly."

"You worry too much, that's your trouble," said Eddie. He had leaned the sword against the side of the box and was now cleaning his fingernails with the tip of his dagger. "By the time they get home they'll have forgotten what happened, but they'll think twice before they try anything with you again, only they won't remember why."

"How could they forget you?" asked Walker. "I mean you're not very forgettable."

"I suppose it's what you would call magic," Eddie replied. "I can make myself visible or invisible at will, and I can make people remember me or have no recollection of ever having seen me."

"No way!" exclaimed Walker. "There's no way you could do that. It's impossible!"

"Well, just you wait and see," replied Eddie. "See if that Daniel guy wants to mess with you next time he meets you. He'll be so scared of you they'll call him Spaniel, not Daniel."

Walker snorted with laughter. The thought of Daniel as a meek dog with floppy ears was so unlike the bully he knew. He watched Eddie as he continued to pick at the dirt beneath his nails with the blade. He was clearly nuts with all his talk of kingdoms and his sword and crazy hat, but then maybe you had to be a bit loony to do magic. Magic had always fascinated Walker—not the stuff conjurers performed at parties, but the kind wizards did, spells and things like that. If there was a chance, even the smallest one, that Eddie was telling the truth . . .

"Really?" said Walker. "You can really do that? Where did you learn a trick like that?"

"It's not a trick," Eddie protested. "It's real magic, and it's easy when you know how."

There was silence while Walker thought about what he just said.

"Could you teach me how to do it?" he asked after a few moments.

"Certainly," said Eddie, looking up from his hands, a sly grin on his face. "But only if you come to the Kingdom."

Walker thought for a moment and then came to his senses. The boy was clearly a liar, and the sooner he went away the better. He would just have to avoid Daniel and his brothers as best he could for the time being.

"Well, maybe," he said, "but not today. Perhaps tomorrow."

Eddie let out a long, frustrated sigh.

"Okay," he said. "If that's the way it's got to be, but get here at the same time. Don't be late, or I'll come looking for you."

And he vanished into thin air.

Walker stood for a long time looking at the spot where Eddie had been. There was no way he could have disappeared, but he had, leaving no trace.

Later on, when Walker was in his bedroom about to go to sleep, he checked through all his books that dealt with the subject of magic. One of his favorites was called *The Necromancer's Almanac*, and it covered everything from alchemy to voodoo, but nowhere could he find any reference to a kingdom called Nebula. He started to leaf through a book on wizards when his mother opened the bedroom door.

"Time to turn the light out, honey," she said. "I know there's no school tomorrow, but it's really late."

"Okay, Mom," he replied. "Good night."

"Good night, sweetie. Sleep well."

As he lay there in the dark, he thought about Eddie. Maybe he was just nuts, or some weird practical joker. But then maybe, just maybe, he did know magic. Walker would love to have the ability to make people forget they had ever seen him. That way nobody would remember the ugly mark on his face. That would be so cool, and if he could master that, who knew what else he might be able to do?

He would call the boy's bluff, tell him that he wanted to go to the Kingdom, and then see what happened. If it *was* nothing, as Walker suspected would be the case, then at least he would know that the boy was a fraud. But if he really could do magic and there really was a place called Nebula . . . well, that would be something else altogether.

CHAPTER 3

The following morning Walker's mother was baking in the kitchen. She looked up and smiled at him as he entered, her hands and apron covered in flour. A smear of it was on her forehead where she had brushed the hair out of her eyes.

"Good morning," she said. "What are you going to do today?"

His mother cut the pastry for the top of the pie, frowning with concentration as she worked.

"Nothing much," said Walker.

"You know, even though I like having you watch me bake," said his mother, "wouldn't you rather be out on a lovely day like today playing with someone your own age? I wish you had more friends."

"I do," Walker assured her. "I have a new friend. I met him yesterday."

"You did?" said his mother. "That's wonderful. What's his name? Why didn't you bring him home? I'd like to meet him."

"Well . . ." Walker shuffled his feet uncomfortably.

"Ah," said his mother. Then, after a pause, she asked, "Is he a real friend or another imaginary one?" Mrs. Watson had experience of Walker making up friends as a substitute for the real thing.

"No, he's real, all right."

"Tell me all about him. What he's like?" urged his mother.

"Well, he says he's a prince," Walker replied, "and he has a huge sword and a dagger and a Red Sox jacket."

"I see" was all Walker's mother said, and she lifted up the top of the pie and carefully put it in place. Feeling a little foolish, he mumbled something to her about playing in the backyard, and after he left the house he ambled down the path toward his box.

Why had he said anything about Eddie at all? He would probably never see the boy again, and yet he kept on thinking about what Eddie had said and the way he had vanished. Thoughts about the stranger were filling so much of his mind that he couldn't concentrate on his book, so he sat on the stone wall that the box was wedged against, kicking his legs backward and forward.

Suddenly he saw a dim shape shimmering in the air in front of him. At first it was just a faint outline, but it got more solid and more real the closer it came. It was Eddie! He was traveling at speed and almost crashed into Walker and the wall, causing his fedora to tilt at an awkward angle. His sword waved dangerously in the air as he tried to balance himself.

"Whoa!" he cried. "I think I overdid it a bit, but I was in a hurry. We have some things we have to do before we can go to the Kingdom, so I'm glad you're on time."

Eddie was already striding off toward the barn at the back of the yard, leaving Walker to run after him to catch up.

"What sort of things?" Walker inquired.

"We have to make an entry point," Eddie said, "in order to transport you. Me, I can just pop in and out as I please, but for a human it's a bit trickier."

"What do you mean, 'for a human'?" Walker asked him. "Aren't you human? You look it—more or less."

"Yes, well, 'more or less' pretty much describes it," Eddie agreed. "I sort of am and am not. But it would take way too much time to explain it to you now. We have things to do and they'll take a little effort."

The effort turned out to be neither little nor Eddie's. He led them around to the back of the barn, a rickety old structure that was now mostly used to store garden tools and Mr. Watson's lawn tractor. When they were out of view from the house Eddie instructed Walker to get a spade.

"What do we need a spade for?" he asked.

"We've got to dig a hole to get you started," Eddie answered.

"Why?" asked Walker.

"Dig and you'll soon find out," Eddie assured him.

"I have to dig my way to this kingdom of yours?" Walker said. "I don't think so! It doesn't sound very magical to me. If you really were a wizard you could make the hole appear by itself. But then, if you really, really were a wizard we wouldn't need a hole in the first place."

"I never said I was a wizard," Eddie protested. "I said

I knew some magic, which I do, but like everything else magic needs preparation and preparation often involves hard work, so start digging."

"Why do I have to dig?" Walker asked. "What's wrong with you starting?"

"You're the one who wants to go there," Eddie replied.

"No, I'm not," Walker reminded him. "You're the one who wants to take me there. I could care less."

Actually this wasn't altogether true. Walker was starting to get curious about this kingdom. And the way Eddie had vanished yesterday and reappeared today— there must be some magic in that. There *must* be!

And so, when it was clear for whatever reason that Eddie wasn't going to lift a finger, he reluctantly began to dig. After about half an hour there was a fairly large hole. Walker rested on the spade and wiped the sweat from his forehead with a muddy hand.

"Come on," Eddie exhorted him. "There's no time to be resting."

"Resting seems to be working fine for you," said Walker. "As far as I'm concerned this is a perfectly good hole, and I'm not going to dig anymore."

Eddie sighed, lifted the front of his fedora, and scratched his head.

"Well," he said, "I guess it will have to do."

He took Walker's hand and they both stood on the rim. The hole wasn't very impressive, Walker had to admit, but he was determined to do no more if Eddie wasn't prepared to help.

"I'm going to count to three, and then we jump in together," Eddie said.

"No way," Walker protested. "Not until you tell me why!"

"You are such a pain," Eddie replied. "Why is because if you don't jump you're going to wish you had for the rest of your life."

"If I don't jump, how will I know?" he asked.

"That's precisely my point," said Eddie, and then he leapt into the hole, pulling Walker after him.

King Leukos sighed. He was very old, and right now he felt it as he watched one of his favorite knights talking to a page.

Everyone, he thought, *is so much younger than me, and so innocent of the dangers that surround us.*

But his age was only one of his worries, and not even the most troublesome.

"My lord Jevon," he commanded, with the clear tone of

one who was used to being obeyed. The knight turned toward him.

"Your Majesty?" he replied.

"I have not seen Lady Lumina," the king said. "Do you know where she is?"

"Yes, sire," Jevon replied. "I believe she has organized jousting games for the Lightkeepers in the meadows next to the farm."

"Games!" cried the king in a despairing voice. "All anyone seems to do around here is play games. We're facing the biggest threat to the safety of this kingdom in many Eons, and my Lightkeepers play games."

"Lady Lumina thinks it is a way for us all to hone our fighting skills," the knight assured him.

"Prancing around on overbred unicorns waving lances at one another isn't going to scare either the Black Count or the Warriors of the Black Shroud, I can assure you of that," said the king. "And if everyone's honing their fighting skills, why aren't you with them?"

"It's my turn to command the royal guard, sire," the knight replied.

"Well in that case, get that boy—what's his name?" asked the king, pointing to the page.

"Astrodor, sire," Jevon informed him.

"Get him to come over here. I have a task for him to do," the king ordered.

Jevon went over to get the page, while the king sat on his throne, a worried expression deepening the lines on his already wrinkled face. When Jevon returned with the page the monarch stood up and put his hands on the boy's shoulders.

"Now listen here, Astrodor," the king said. "I have an important mission for you. Do you have a unicorn?"

"No, Your Majesty," Astrodor replied.

"The boy can use mine, sire," Jevon assured the king. "He's tethered in the courtyard."

"Very good," said the king. "Now I want you to ride like the blazes to the meadows by the unicorn farm and tell Lady Lumina that the king commands her and all the Lightkeepers to attend him at the Palace immediately."

"Yes, sire," said Astrodor. "At once."

The page was so excited either by his mission or the prospect of riding Jevon's unicorn that he turned and ran from the room instead of slowly walking backward as was the customary way of leaving the king's presence.

"Oh, for the energy of youth," remarked the king as he watched the boy disappear.

"Yes, Your Majesty," said Jevon. "A wonderful thing, but I think I prefer the wisdom of age."

"Wisdom without action is worthless," the king told his knight, "and action demands energy. I sometimes wonder if I have enough of either to guide my people through these perilous times."

"You have the vitality of men half your age, sire, and you've never let your people down," Jevon said.

"In one way I have," replied the king. "I have no successor, no heir to take over my responsibilities when the time comes. That is a failure, in my opinion. And speaking of successors, isn't Prince Edward due to return about now? Where's Luzaro?"

The king clapped his hands to summon his servant. The curtains at the far end of the chamber parted and through them came a tall, dignified man.

"Your majesty?" he asked in a quiet voice.

"Luzaro," said the king, "is there any news of Prince Edward?"

"I believe he has just arrived, Your Majesty," Luzaro assured him, "and he's in the company of an Outer-worlder. They should be in the palace shortly."

"Please show them both in as soon as they get here," said the king.

"Very good, sire," replied his servant, and he left the room.

The king sighed. The boy had brought him many candidates from the Outerworld, but none of them had been right. Eddie's latest claim to have found the perfect contender did not fill the king with any optimism.

"Time is short," he said to himself. "This has to be the one."

Eddie was clearly in a hurry. As soon as Walker was steady on his feet the prince took him by the hand and started to bustle his way through the crowds of people on the streets. When the passersby saw the mark on Walker's cheek they turned to stare, but not in the way Walker was used to. They seemed to be looking at a precious object they had never seen before. But the thing that struck Walker with the greatest force, and that washed away his fear of being in this strange place, was the energy he could feel. It was almost as if the very air charged him like he was a battery, and he felt invincible.

Eddie turned on to what appeared to be the main avenue, a road divided by a center strip of grass. On it at regular intervals were statues of men and women, each holding a shining round orb in the right hand. When

Walker looked to the left he could see in the far distance a huge pair of gates set into the city walls. To the right the broad thoroughfare led up to the castle. Eddie had let go of his hand and was striding toward it at a rapid pace. Walker had to grab hold of his Red Sox jacket to slow him down.

"Eddie, where are we going?" he demanded.

"To the palace." Eddie nodded toward the large building. "You have an appointment with the king, and he doesn't like to be kept waiting."

"Why would the king want to see me?" Walker asked.

"Everything will be revealed when we get there," Eddie replied. "All I can say is you'd better get used to being called 'my lord.'"

CHAPTER 4

The palace was smaller than it had first appeared from the outside, no more than two or three stories tall. There were no windows, just openings in the walls at irregular intervals, and wide staircases leading to the upper floors. Everything was made of bronze-colored stone that looked metallic at first glance, but was apparently soft and crumbly. Whenever someone brushed against it a cloud of fine dust drifted into the air. Eddie noticed Walker looking at this, and seemed to read his thoughts.

"Don't worry," he said. "I've seen it do that for hundreds of years. It's not going to collapse anytime soon."

Walker looked at his strange companion. The boy appeared to be no more than ten, eleven at the most. How could he know what the building had been like for so long? This was a question that would have to be answered later, for Eddie was now striding toward a staircase that led to a square tower. Walker had to run to catch up to him.

"Wait for me!" he cried. "Where are we going?"

"I told you," Eddie replied. "To see the king."

There were no lamps on the staircase. It relied on the glow from the walls for light. They had climbed up two levels of the tower when they came upon a soft rope hooked across the stairway. The rope looked as if it was made of spun gold, and to one side of it a notice was posted.

Citizens of the Kingdom of Nebula,
These stairs lead to
The Royal Apartments.
You are requested to respect them
And only enter upon urgent business
With the King.

Code of Light Section 3 Subsection 24

Eddie unhooked one end of the shimmering rope and held it to let Walker pass through.

"Are we allowed to come in here? Isn't it just for royals?" Walker asked, glancing at the notice.

"We *are* royalty. Why would we not be allowed into the Royal Apartments?" Eddie replied.

"Well, you might be," said Walker, "but I'm not. In my country we don't have royalty."

"You're not in your country," Eddie pointed out, "and things are a little different here. Actually a lot different," he added.

At the top the stairway opened onto a large, bare room decorated with huge paintings of a terrible battle. Warriors dressed in silver armor, just like the knight on the unicorn that Walker had seen earlier, were fighting huge giants whose faces were covered by heavy black shrouds. Despite the difference in their size the smaller fighters seemed to be winning. Their massive catapults heaved gleaming balls into the air, while riders threw lances that shone brightly in the dark landscape. The giants were in retreat, some stumbling over the bodies of their fallen comrades. Walker was so fascinated by these decorations that he did not notice a man come into the room from behind a curtain.

"Welcome back, Your Royal Highness," he said. "I trust your mission was successful?"

"I think so, Luzaro, but that's for His Majesty to decide," Eddie said.

As if to confirm this, a bellowing sound came from the other side of the drape.

"Am I to wait here for another Eon until you decide to bring them in?" roared the king. "What's the point of being king, I ask you, if people take their own sweet time to do what you tell them?"

Luzaro looked at Eddie and smiled a conspiratorial smile.

"I think we should go in, don't you?" he said.

Eddie nodded, and Luzaro threw back the curtain to reveal a room full of people, many of them dressed in mirrored armor. At the far end was the source of all the commotion—the king. He was seated on an enormous, shining throne, but rose to his feet as they entered. Before the two boys could go forward to meet him, a short, worried-looking little man ran up, an enormous book cradled in his arms and an old-fashioned quill pen in one hand.

"Just one moment, boys," he said. "I have to get a few

details from our Outerworld friend before we go any farther."

"Fussingham," roared the king, "will you go away and leave us alone!"

"But, sire," complained the little man, "I have to record the time and details of this meeting, as well as the young man's name and particulars. It's for the Book of the Kingdom." He offered the book up to the sovereign as if in evidence.

"If you don't vanish immediately," shouted the king, "you'll also be recording the time of your banishment from the royal household and the details of your new employment in the stone quarry!"

With almost a squeal the book's custodian scurried away.

"Never was a man more aptly named than Fussingham," sighed the king. "Come here, boy; come here and let me have a look at you."

The King was obviously very old, but even from across the room Walker could see that he was still powerful. He was tall, straight, and looked very strong. He was also someone used to giving orders and having them obeyed, and it never occurred to Walker not to do as he was told. The two boys moved toward him, and as they did the knights parted to let them through. When they were within a few feet of the throne the king hurried toward them.

"Let's see what you've brought me this time," he said to Eddie.

Then he went up to Walker, took his chin in his hand, and turned the right side of the boy's head toward him. He looked at the mark on Walker's cheekbone and a triumphant smile broke out across his face.

"Finally!" he shouted. "Finally you've brought me a true Chosen One. I knew there must be one in all the Outerworld."

He then took Walker's hand in his own, led him to the throne, sat down, and looked Walker straight in the eye. The boy saw that the king's eyes shone like Eddie's.

"Now listen carefully to me, young man," the king began. "You should know how important you being here today is to this small Kingdom. We have looked for someone like you for Eons, or hundreds of your Outerworld years. That mark you bear on your face means that your destiny is to rule this realm and to be its king when I pass on. Our messenger here"—he nodded toward Eddie—"has brought me many candidates. You are the only one who bears the true mark of a Chosen One. You will learn, as we get to know each other, how important that is, but for now sit next to me while I conduct some rather tiresome business with these people here. Luzaro, bring the young lord a chair."

Walker felt panic rising up in his chest. All he could think about was a story he had seen recently on TV. It was about a boy who had been kidnapped and held until his father paid a ransom to his captors. Walker's situation seemed far worse than that. He had allowed himself to be abducted by Eddie because of his stupid curiosity and for the sake of a few magic tricks, and now he was trapped in an alien world in the power of a king who would keep him there to be the next ruler. His captor wasn't interested in money or anything else his parents might hand over in exchange for Walker's freedom. The king was only interested in the hateful mark on Walker's face.

Walker knew that he had to stay calm. His one hope was to persuade Eddie to take him back. It was unlikely the boy would do it willingly, given that he had apparently spent so long looking for someone like Walker, but maybe Walker could trick him into returning. Maybe he could say that he had left something behind that he needed, or that he wanted to say good-bye to his parents.

That he might never see them again was too painful to even think about. Somehow he *had* to trick Eddie into taking him back, and once there he would fill in the hole in the garden and that would be an end to it. For the moment, however, it was vital that he appear to cooperate with the king's plans, so he sat in the chair Luzaro had brought for him and listened to what was going on.

The king was striding up and down declaring in a loud voice that a group called the Warriors of the Black Shroud was on the move and that there wasn't a moment to be lost in preparing for the defense of the Kingdom. It was clear to Walker even in his frightened state that the others were uncomfortable with what the king was saying. Some of them looked down at their feet in an embarrassed way, and the less they heeded him the louder the king became.

"The last patrol that tried to get through to Litherium disappeared completely!" he yelled. "We still don't know what has happened to them. They could all be dead or enslaved by now while we listen to minstrels and watch jugglers and do nothing."

A tall, dignified woman walked forward to address the king. She had cropped white hair and wore waist-length armor over a long, flowing white gown with a short gold-trimmed cape on top of it all. She was not a young woman, but like the king she projected the energy and power of someone more youthful. For the first time Walker noticed that the armor that appeared to be made of metal was flexible and moved with the wearer, bending its form to her body.

"Your majesty," she began, "even though you haven't been outside the walls in some time you will probably remember that there are often unusual weather conditions in Diabolonia that make travel difficult."

"Lumina," said the king, more quietly now but just as determinedly, "I may be older than you but my memory is still sound and I know of no weather conditions so unusual that they can make an entire patrol disappear. I also remember that the Black Count swore revenge when we defeated him at the Battle of Barren Plains, and although that was several Eons ago I know that he hasn't forgotten either."

"He may not have forgotten, sire," Lumina continued, "but he hasn't the resources to defeat us. He didn't then and he hasn't now."

"Resources!" exploded the king, back to full shouting mode. "What resources would he need? Just look at what's in front of me. These are the Lightkeepers, my

Warrior Class, the Defenders of the Realm. When was the last time any of them fought? In fact, how many of them have fought at all? Only you, Lumina, have ever been in battle, you and the child warrior over there, and he's been cursed for eternity."

Eddie shifted about awkwardly when the king said this.

"And how much training have they done?" the king continued. "And I don't count these jousting parties you organize from time to time. No, you mark my words, Lumina, we would be defenseless against any attack the Black Shroud could bring. Our only hope is that the Sister Cities are better prepared than we are."

Lumina stood in front of the king, her head bowed. She then raised it and looked the monarch straight in the eyes.

"Your majesty," she continued, "because of the bravery and sacrifices of you and your knights of old we have had peace in the Kingdom for as long as any of its citizens have been alive. You are right when you say that I am the only one of the Lightkeepers who lived through those days of fear and sorrow, and the terror that almost came to the walls of our homes. I have seen death and mourning, and I do not want to visit those places again. But I have also seen the casualties we inflicted upon our enemies. You remember the Black Count vowing revenge; I remember him fleeing in humiliation. I do not believe that after all these years he will attack us again. If we leave him alone he will remain in the deep wastes of Diabolonia, but if we provoke him he will defend himself and then the beasts that surround him will be enraged and the nightmares of the past will return. I most strongly advise you, sire, not to let that happen. Let our sons, daughters, brothers, and sisters enjoy the fruits of the peace that you and your comrades fought so hard for."

There was a murmur of approval among the crowd at the end of Lumina's speech, and from the expression on his face the king was not happy.

"I could do as you say and ignore the threat beyond the Kingdom's walls," he said, "but what about those within our boundaries? What about the Nightangels?"

"Nightangels, sire?" The king's remark caught Lumina by surprise. "It never occurred to me that Nightangels might actually exist. I always looked upon them as make-believe creatures used to scare disobedient children."

"No, Lumina," said the king. "They exist."

"What evidence is there of their presence then, sire?" Lumina asked. "I see none. Most of our people are happy and content, but they will not remain so for long if they sense that their leaders live in fear."

The king looked around at the assembly and then turned his attention to Walker.

"Well, Chosen One," he said, "what do you think?"

Walker said nothing for a few moments, and then he blurted out something he had been determined not to say.

"Please—I want to go home!"

CHAPTER 5

If Walker had been able to catch the words and stuff them back into his mouth he would have. But it was too late. Everyone had heard them. He looked around, frightened, but even the fearsome-looking Lumina softened her expression a little, and the king seemed almost as if he was in pain.

"My dear boy," he said, "we have treated you so badly; you must forgive us. We have looked for so long for a Chosen One, and have had so many disappointments, that we forgot, in our joy and relief at finding you, that you are a person and have a life, and what we want may not be what you want."

Lumina looked at him and smiled a sympathetic smile.

"The mark," she said, "grants you the ability to rule, but unless you have the will to rule it is as if you were a commoner."

"Lumina is right," the king agreed. "And I have faith that you shall have the will when you understand more of this realm. Come with me and I will explain many things to you. Lightkeepers, we must continue our discussion at a later date, but not too much later."

He took Walker by the hand and walked behind the throne. Eddie made as if to accompany them, and the king turned toward him.

"No, young prince," he said gently. "This is only for Chosen Ones. I will reunite you with him when we are finished."

"Very well, sire," said Eddie.

It was at this moment that Walker looked up into the king's face. There, in the same place as on Walker's cheekbone, was an identical star-shaped birthmark. The king pulled open the drape that concealed his bedchamber. The room was very simple and mostly bare of furniture, but there was an enormous bed on a raised platform.

The only decoration was a carving of an ancient heraldic shield on the wall opposite the entrance. The king took Walker over to the bed and sat down on it, indicating that the boy should be seated on a stone bench nearby. He was silent for a few moments as if he was trying to work out the best way to tell Walker something.

"When I see fine young men like you," he finally began, "I always wish that I had been blessed with children of my own, but unfortunately it was not to be. If I had a son or daughter I would have passed the mark on to them, and then this search for a Chosen One that has gone on for so long would not have been necessary, and you wouldn't be here now.

"I don't know why you got the mark," the king continued after a couple of minutes. "But I do know what it means. It means that if you choose to you could lead this Kingdom when I have gone. It shows that you have the strength to do so—not the physical strength, but the strength to do the right thing and to care for your people, to put their interests ahead of your own, and if necessary put your own life second to theirs. I hope I can persuade you that this is something you not only could do but that you will do."

"But I don't live here," Walker protested. "I don't even

come from here. I have a family in another world. I couldn't rule here and live there."

"In fact," said the king, "you could. Time here and where you come from have little relationship to each other. You could stay here for many Eons, and become an old man like me, and then return to the Outerworld and it would be as if you had been gone for two of your— what do you call them?—your seconds. You would go back to being a boy—how old are you in Outerworld time?"

"Eleven," said Walker.

"Well!" the king cried triumphantly. "You would be an eleven-year-old again. Now wouldn't that be something worth having! I would love to be your age again."

Walker looked at the old, old man with his papery skin and ancient gnarled hands, and it was impossible to believe that he had ever been eleven. He felt sorry for him. Even his Lightkeepers didn't want to hear his predictions of disaster. As far as Walker could see the king didn't have anyone on his side. Walker felt the same way at school, but he could come home to his mother and his books. Then the king took the boy's hands in his own, and looked him straight in the face as if he had come to a decision.

"I'm going to take you to a place where only Chosen Ones may go," he said. "It is called the Source, and it is where all of the energy for the Kingdom is stored. Without it we would be doomed to live forever in darkness, and our enemies would overwhelm us, for the dark is what they know the best."

"You mean it's like a generator?" asked Walker.

"I do not know what that is," replied the king, "but what I do know is that there is nothing like it in the Outerworld. You have seen nothing like the Source, and in fact nobody in the Kingdom apart from myself has ever seen anything like it. You and I are the only ones who can be in its presence."

"Why?" Walker inquired.

"That I cannot tell you," the king said. "In fact, much of what you see you will not remember, for the Source has secrets that only a ruler can know, and until you decide that you will be the future king, these secrets must remain hidden from you. Only when you truly commit to that will you be able to remember them. You will even forget how we got to the Source and how we returned, for its location is one of the greatest secrets."

"You can do that?" asked Walker. "You can really make people forget things?"

"Of course," replied the king with a smile. "It's one of the most useful things I know."

"And can Eddie—I mean Prince Edward—do that as well?"

"I would hope so," said the king, "for I taught him myself many Eons ago."

"Wow," said Walker.

And then suddenly it was as if he was dreaming, one of those dreams where you know more or less what is happening but the details are unclear. He knew they were going down brightly lit tunnels, and he saw walls sliding open to reveal the rooms behind them. Then all at once they were standing in a large round chamber, on the walls of which hung lances similar to the one the knight on the unicorn had been carrying. The room itself had no floor as such, but a series of circular steps that went up several feet. These ended in a platform on which was a carving of a claw. Nestled within the claw sat a globe, no bigger than a basketball, that shone brighter than the brightest light he had ever seen. He could feel the enormous power that flowed from it. A crown of exquisite workmanship hovered a few feet above, suspended from the roof by delicate metal cables. Energy pulsed up and down these lines, crackling and sparking. It was as if the crown was gathering up the orb's energy and transmitting it through the cables.

"This is the Source," said the king in a quiet voice, as if they were in a sacred place. "We are standing in the Sanctuary, the most secret location in the Kingdom. There is also another secret that I must tell you that I pray you may never need to use, and that is . . . "

And then Walker's brain went all fuzzy, and the next thing he knew he was sitting back on the stone bench by the king's bed, with the monarch bending over him.

"How do you feel?" the king asked.

"Amazing," Walker replied. "I have so much energy, I feel as if I could do anything I wanted to, anything in the world."

"And you could!" cried the king. "Well, anything in this world anyway. That's the gift of the Source to a Chosen One, the ability to absorb some of its power and use it for the good of the people. Come now, let us take a walk outside."

The king pulled back the curtain that separated the bedroom from the antechamber, and the buzz of conversation from the Lightkeepers ceased as the monarch entered the room.

"Lightkeepers," said the king, "the Chosen One and I

are going to take a quick tour of the Kingdom, so you are dismissed for now. We will reassemble in the next cycle and discuss the security situation further. Now where's that messenger? Prince Edward, show yourself immediately!"

"I'm here, sire," said Eddie, who was standing right behind the king.

"For the love of light!" the king exclaimed. "Don't go creeping up on people like that! It's most unnerving, especially when you're carrying that overgrown carving knife of yours. Do you have to have it constantly? Couldn't you leave it somewhere?"

He was referring to Eddie's sword, and Walker saw a look of determination spread over the boy's face. The King noticed it too.

"No, I suppose since you've been hauling it around for Eons it's probably with you for eternity," he said. "Come along. I want to show my young lord here what he's been missing by living in the Outerworld."

"Very good, sire," Eddie said, and the three of them left the palace.

As they walked through the streets it became clear to Walker that the king was a man beloved by his people. Wherever they went the citizens greeted them with smiles and friendly waves, the men bowing and the women curtsying as he passed. It was also clear that the king loved his people and his Kingdom with equal passion. He was excited like a child to show both to Walker, and the boy realized that probably very few strangers ever passed that way, if any.

"See here," cried the king as they passed a small workshop. "Look at this fellow. Look at that necklace he's making. Have you ever seen finer craftsmanship? Beautiful stuff. We love jewelry here; it reflects the light, you see."

Whatever they saw the king assured Walker that it was unequaled in its excellence, not just in Nebula but on any planet anywhere in the universe. The king challenged Walker to prove him wrong, which, of course, he couldn't. They had just turned onto one of the avenues from a side street when a boy crashed into Walker, sending him flying to the ground.

"Oh, my lord," he cried. "I'm so sorry. I was in a hurry and didn't look where I was going? Are you hurt?"

"Young man, have you ever heard of the word 'walk'?" the king asked crossly.

"Yes, sire, I have," replied the boy. "But I always seem to end up running."

By this time Walker was back on his feet. The boy began to brush the dust that was everywhere in Nebula off Walker's clothes.

"I didn't mean to do that. I'm Astrodor, by the way." He held out his hand for Walker to shake, and then for the first time he looked up at Walker's face and was transfixed.

"Oh wow," he said in awe. "The mark of the Chosen One. Can I touch it?"

Instinctively Walker turned his head away. The king crouched down and looked straight into his eyes.

"Don't ever be ashamed of that mark," he said, quietly but seriously. "Do you realize how few faces in history have been adorned with it? Only a handful of people have been so privileged. Be grateful for it. Show it with pride."

But the king was wrong. Walker hadn't turned his face away because he was ashamed of his birthmark. Eddie had said the mark meant Walker was royalty. Astrodor looked at it with awe. The king claimed it made Walker a leader. But Walker knew none of it was true. He was just a wimpy kid with no friends, nothing special, no matter what anyone thought. And he didn't like anyone looking at him as if he was. It made him feel ashamed, not of the mark, but of himself.

The king strode on, shaking his subjects' hands and pointing out this feature and that. Walker had to almost run to catch him up. Although they must have walked for hours he didn't feel the slightest bit tired. Then the tour was over and they were back at the palace.

"Well, Chosen One," the king said, "I hope that you enjoyed our little trip around this realm. These are good people, for the most part. Their only fault is that they have lived at peace for so long that they have forgotten that the powers of evil do not rest. But this is a fault most people would happily be burdened with, and not one of their own making."

He paused, and then put his hands on Walker's shoulders.

"And now," he said, "it is time for you to go home. Now you must return to the Outerworld."

CHAPTER 6

Walker couldn't believe his ears. Was the king really going to allow him to go back and leave the Kingdom behind? Didn't he understand that Walker would never return? The king smiled at him as if he knew everything that Walker was thinking.

"Why would I send you back to the Outerworld?" he said. "The better question is: Why would I keep you here against your will? What possible good would it do the Kingdom to have you here longing to be somewhere else? No, you must go back if for no other reason than to realize that time spent in the Kingdom in no way affects time in the Outerworld. Prince Edward will take you whenever you wish, and he will bring you back when you feel you are ready—if you feel you are ready."

"I think I'm ready to leave," said Walker, not wanting to let the opportunity to return home slip from his grasp.

"In that case," said the king, "you must go. Prince Edward, take your friend to the Outerworld, and keep an eye on him while he's there. He is, after all, a Chosen One, and deserves our protection."

"I will, sire," Eddie replied.

The king turned to Walker and shook his hand. "Good-bye, young man. Until we meet again, which I hope will be soon."

Walker said good-bye to the king and to the Lightkeepers as he and Eddie made their way out of the palace. They walked along the wide avenue that led to the gates of the Kingdom. Eddie suddenly took Walker's hand and started running. Then everything went black and the next thing he knew the two of them tumbled to a halt in the meadow behind the barn. Walker was facedown in the long grass, and he looked up to see Eddie rolling over and over, his Boston Red Sox jacket covered in burrs. He finally stopped with a thump against an apple tree.

"Oooph," was all he could say.

He picked up his battered fedora and brushed the leaves and dirt off it.

"I really have to work on my reentry skills," he said.

"When will you go back to the Kingdom?" Walker asked.

"Well," Eddie replied, "I thought I might stick around here for a while. I don't want you forgetting about us."

"That would be pretty hard," Walker said.

"Unless I make you forget," Eddie retorted with a grin.

"Yeah," said Walker. "You never did show me how to do that!"

"We can't let you into all of our secrets all at once," Eddie replied. "If we did you'd never come back."

Walker felt a pang of conscience when Eddie said that, because, in his heart of hearts, he knew he never would.

"It'd be fun to have you around," he told him, and surprisingly he meant it.

"Well, say hi to your mom for me," said Eddie, "and tell her to save a slice of that cherry pie she's making."

And with that he disappeared.

How does he know my mom's making a cherry pie? Walker wondered to himself.

When he got back to the house, his mother was still in the kitchen. Walker's nose detected the comforting smell of a pie baking in the oven. He went up to her, kissed her on the cheek, and then sat down on one of the kitchen chairs.

"Did you miss me?" he asked.

"No," she replied. "Why would I miss you? You must've been gone all of two minutes. Much as I love you I can bear to be apart from you for that amount of time."

So, he thought, *it really does work like the king said it would. There is a difference between time here and in the Kingdom.*

"You look pretty perky today," his mother said. "You've got a sort of glow about you."

When she said that Walker froze. Could it be that the effects of being in the Kingdom didn't wear off immediately? He stole a furtive glance at his hands, but they looked just like they always did when he was home.

"Since you told me you don't have any plans for the rest of this lovely day I've arranged a surprise for you," his mother said.

For the second time in as many minutes Walker froze.

"What kind of a surprise?" he asked nervously.

"You know that old cottage on the Trumbell farm?" his mother asked him. "It seems that old Jeremiah Trumbell sold it to some folks from Boston. Anyway, they've been doing it up, and now they've moved in, and they have a daughter. So I invited her to come and play with you. She should be here soon."

"Oh, Mom!" cried Walker. "You know how I hate meeting kids."

"Sweetie, you've got to get over it," his mother insisted. "You can't spend the rest of your life in isolation. You *have* to learn to get along with other people."

"But those Outerworld kids always treat me like a freak," Walker complained.

"What kind of kids?" asked his mother.

"Oh, it's just a word I use to describe people who aren't from around here," Walker hurriedly said.

"Well, you're not a freak," his mother assured him. "You just have a slight blemish that isn't nearly as noticeable as you think it is."

"If it isn't noticeable," Walker replied, "then why is it the first thing about me anyone notices?"

"You're too sensitive." His mother sighed. "Anyway, it's

too late to disinvite her now. She'll be here any moment."

"I'm going up to my room," Walker said crossly. "If you want me that's where I'll be!"

Walker had become skilled at avoiding his mother's attempts to organize social occasions for him. He had developed techniques that often managed to get rid of intruders quickly, and one of them was to present himself as the most boring boy they had ever met. He decided to read a book no other kid would be interested in. He looked around his room; then his eyes stopped on the perfect solution—*Collins English Dictionary and Thesaurus (New Edition)*. He pulled it down from the mantel above the fireplace, settled on his bed, his legs tucked under him, and did his best to look thoroughly interested.

There was a knock on his door and then his mother came in.

"Walker, this is . . ."

And that was as far as she got before Frances Livonia Hayes burst into the tiny bedroom and into his life like a force of nature.

"Hi, I'm Frances, but my friends call me Frankie. You can call me Frankie too if you like, because I think we're going to be friends. I hope so anyway because I love having friends. I've got lots and lots, and I bet you do too."

Walker couldn't believe his eyes or his ears. She was short and skinny, and maybe a year or two younger than he was. She practically crackled with energy and Walker had the feeling she wasn't going to be easy to get rid of.

"What a cool room. It's so old. I love old, don't you? Our house is old too. Not the one in Boston, 'cause that's an apartment, not a house, but the one across the road. I love to imagine all the things that must have happened in each room for all the years before us. Do you think anyone ever died in this room? I bet they did."

Actually this was one of the things that Walker had wondered about, because his bedroom was in the oldest part of the house, but Frankie had already launched into something else.

"What are you reading? A dictionary! I love dictionaries. I spend hours looking at the one we have at home. I love words, don't you? My favorite game is Scrabble— and crosswords. I *love* crosswords. What words are you looking at?"

She took the book from his hands and ran her index finger across the pages.

"Hey, look at this. Phillumenist—a person who collects

matchbox labels. I didn't know matchboxes had labels, did you? Or at least none worth collecting? Don't people do funny things?"

Walker's head started to spin.

"Slow down!" was all he could think to say.

"Oh, I'm sorry," Frankie replied. "My mom always tells me I talk too much, but I tell her it's because I have two lawyers for parents so what does she expect. What's that on your face? Is that a tattoo? That is so cool. I love tats. I *soooo* want one but my mom says I'm too young. Do you think I'm too young for one?"

He was now confused enough that he didn't know what to think. This was the second time in just a few hours that someone had made a virtue out of his hated birthmark. He could understand why the citizens of Nebula thought it was great, but Frankie was just an ordinary girl.

"No—I mean yes," he finally mumbled. "I mean it's not a tattoo. It's a birthmark."

"Wow!" she said, peering more closely. "That's amazing. Will it ever go away?"

"I don't think so," he replied. "I wish it would, but I don't think it will."

"Why would you want it to?" she asked. "It makes you

different and that's so great. I love being different. Why would you ever want to be the same as everyone else? What's the point of that?"

"I dunno," he said, shrugging his shoulders. "Sometimes it just seems easier."

"Oh, please!" she replied.

And that was that, end of conversation, or at least of that topic. Her final word on Walker's birthmark didn't prevent Frankie from discussing the merits of her cell phone when compared to that of her best friend's; her favorite food—meatloaf; her least favorite food—fish because it tasted fishy; her favorite books, movies, cars, card games, skateboards, teachers, and on, and on, and on. The fact that Walker barely said a word didn't worry her in the least. In fact she hardly seemed to notice, because when she looked at the clock beside Walker's bed she suddenly said:

"Oh my gosh! Is that clock right? I have to go home. It's been fun. I like you a lot. Do you like me? Shall I come by again tomorrow? Do you wanna go tracking in the woods? Do you think your mom would let you go?"

Walker could only mumble "Yeah, sure" in response and hope that his answer covered most of her questions. After promising to come by the same time the following day, Frankie bounded out, leaving Walker exhausted but okay. A few minutes later his mother poked her head around the door.

"Well, what did you think of Frances?" she inquired anxiously.

"She's different," he replied, and she certainly was.

CHAPTER 7

Tue to her word, Frankie arrived at exactly the same time the next day. Now she was dressed more comfortably in a pair of shorts, some old sneakers, and a T-shirt that said VAMPIRE IN TRAINING. She asked Walker's mom if it was all right for him to go for a walk with her, but had grabbed his hand and was already heading out of the door before Mrs. Watson had a chance to answer. They went to the bottom of the yard, past the hole in the ground behind the barn, and into the woods at the far end. Walker had always loved the woods because he rarely saw anyone else in them, and he was surprised at how much he liked being there with Frankie. Her constant chatter was soothing, like the buzz of bees on a hot summer's day. They came to a clearing where somebody had made a bench out of two tree stumps and a log. Frankie ran over to it and lay down, her hands clasped behind her head, looking up at the patches of sky between the branches of the trees.

"My mom told me that your mom told her that you don't have any friends," she said without turning to look at him.

"I do so," Walker protested.

"I knew you must," said Frankie. "It would be terrible not to have friends. Who's your best one?"

"Well," Walker replied, pausing for a minute as if he was mentally going through an extensive address book, "my newest is a boy called Eddie."

"Does he live near here?" she asked.

"Sort of," Walker said.

"What do you mean—sort of?" Frankie demanded. "Either he lives near here or he doesn't."

"Well, if you really *have* to know," Walker said, getting irritated by her constant questions, "he actually lives in another world, but you can get to it quickly."

"What do you mean—other world?" exclaimed Frankie.

"It's underground," Walker replied. "At least, I think it is. You get there through a long black tunnel."

"You mean he's like a miner?" asked Frankie, completely confused.

"No, he's a prince and he lives in a Kingdom," Walker replied.

Frankie folded her arms and looked Walker straight in the eyes.

"Walker Watson," she said, "I will believe everything you tell me, because I think you should believe what friends tell you, but if you ever lie to me then it's shame on you, not shame on me."

"I'm not lying," Walker protested. "He's real. I've really seen him."

"No way!" exclaimed Frankie, swinging her legs down from the bench and sitting up. "Are you sure?"

"Pretty sure," said Walker, although he didn't sound too certain.

"Pretty sure," Frankie questioned, "or, like, absolutely sure? Did you actually touch him?"

"Yes, we held hands."

"Why?" Frankie asked.

"To get into the Kingdom," Walker replied. "You have

to hold hands and jump into that hole I dug behind the barn."

"Really?" Frankie said excitedly. "Can anyone do it? If we held hands could we go to the Kingdom?"

" I don't think so," said Walker. "I think you have to be with Eddie."

"Oh, come on," urged Frankie, "I bet you can. Let's try it. Please!"

Walker was about to explain to her that he didn't want to go back to the Kingdom but Frankie was already running toward the barn.

"It's not very deep," she observed, looking into the hole.

"No," agreed Walker, "it doesn't have to be. It gets deeper when you jump in."

"Cool!" she cried. "Let's do it."

She grabbed his hand and leaped in, pulling him with her. There was a jarring thud as their feet hit the dirt, and they both tumbled over. She got up and brushed herself off. Walker was relieved that he wasn't on his way back to Nebula because he would have to explain to everyone that he wasn't there because he wanted to be king, but because a girl had pulled him into the hole against his will. It would have been kind of embarrassing.

"Well," Frankie said with a grin, "I guess you're right. We need Eddie. How do you get hold of him?"

"Actually," said Walker, "he gets hold of me. I don't know how to get hold of him."

"What kind of a friend is that?" Frankie exclaimed. "Now that you're my friend you will always be able to get me. Can't you text him or something?"

Walker mumbled something about Eddie not being a texting kind of guy, then got out of the hole and started to walk back toward his house. Frankie quickly caught up with him.

"Don't worry, he'll come back," she said, "and when he does, come get me. I'm going to be here for weeks and weeks, practically forever, so we've got time. I want to go to that Kingdom place with you."

It wasn't until Frankie had gone home and Walker was alone that he thought about what she said. It was true that he had no way of contacting Eddie, and Walker was probably just a job to him. An assignment. One Chosen One—find and deliver ASAP.

That night Walker had a strange dream—two strange dreams, in fact. The first one was really a nightmare. He was walking by himself in an empty, barren place and it was almost dark. There were no trees or shrubs, no

64

buildings, no roads, just an endless flat expanse of rough, stony ground. Suddenly out of this wasteland came the most awful monsters—hooded giants that loomed over him, and skeletons with round, bulging eyes and ragged clothes that flew above him on black-feathered wings. They swept down like angry jackdaws, and he dropped to the ground to avoid them. As he did so, huge, blind black worms rose up out of the arid earth and crawled around his legs and arms, pulling him down so that he could not escape. It took all his strength to free himself from their slimy grasp, and when he was finally upright the skeletons dove toward him again, forcing him back down to the ground, where the worms trapped him once more. He woke up with his heart pounding.

He was convinced that he wouldn't be able to go back to sleep, but no sooner had he thought this than he was dreaming again. Now he was mounted on a gleaming white unicorn, a proud animal with a long, flowing mane, and it walked with great dignity through cheering crowds that thronged the streets of the Kingdom. Riding next to him on his right side was Eddie astride a similarly magnificent animal, only this one was a creamy color. The young prince held his sword aloft. Walker suddenly realized there were arms around his waist, and that he was not alone on the unicorn. He looked over his shoulder and there was Frankie. She winked at him.

"See?" she said. "I told you we could do it. Aren't you glad now you brought me with you?"

The two animals made their way down the long avenue to the courtyard of the palace. The king's empty throne stood in the middle of the yard with the stern figure of Lumina behind it. The two unicorns stopped, waiting for their riders to dismount, when suddenly white wings sprouted from the shoulders of the one ridden by Walker and Frankie, and the animal began to rise in the air. Walker looked down to see Eddie watching them and grinning. Up and up the unicorn flew and the Kingdom got smaller and smaller until it could no longer be seen. They flew into clouds and one of them formed itself into the face of the king. He smiled at the two children.

"All is well," the cloud said. Then Walker woke up and it was morning.

He dressed quickly and went down for his breakfast.

"My, you look full of vim and vigor," his mother observed.

"Yeah, I'm good," Walker said. "I think I'll go and see if Frankie's around."

"I'm so glad you like her," his mother said. "She

seems like a lot of fun."

But it wasn't the prospect of seeing his new friend that had energized him. In fact he wasn't sure why he felt so invigorated, but he thought it had something to do with the dreams, even the bad one. He set out for Frankie's house, but then decided to go by way of the orchard to see if any apples were ripe yet. He rounded the corner of the barn and there was Eddie.

"So," the prince said, leaning his hands and his chin upon the handle of his sword, "you've got yourself a girlfriend, have you? You *are* a lucky lad."

"She's not my girlfriend," Walker protested. "She's just a friend. Anyway, how do you know about her?"

"Ah well," said Eddie mysteriously, "I know a lot of things—not that it does me much good when I have to deal with a stubborn fellow like you. It's all very frustrating. Here I find the one person who can help save the Kingdom after centuries of looking, and you don't want to be king—why not, I can't imagine. Most people would kill to be king; in fact I know some who have. Then I come back to the Outerworld to find you cavorting around with some girl."

"I wasn't cavorting," Walker protested. He wasn't quite sure what cavorting involved, but he was pretty certain that neither he nor Frankie had been doing it. "She's just my friend—the first friend I've ever had."

"I know, I'm sorry," Eddie said, his shoulders suddenly slumping in despair. "I'm sure she's great, but don't you see? The Kingdom may be in peril, and if it goes down, if the Black Shroud triumphs and the Source is extinguished, then my last hope for redemption goes with it and I will be lost for eternity."

"You'll be what?" said Walker.

"Nothing," the young prince replied. "I'm just worried, not just for myself but for all those good people in the Kingdom. Anyway, you've known me longer than you've known her so if anybody's going to be your friend it should be me."

Walker was amazed that Eddie thought of him as a friend, but shocked at what else he said.

"Whoa. Back up a bit. What do you mean—if the Source is extinguished?"

"Like the king said, after the Black Count was defeated at the Battle of Barren Plains he swore revenge," Eddie replied. "He vowed to destroy the Source, because if that goes we go with it. Light is the only defense we have and without it the Warriors of the Black Shroud would destroy the Kingdom and enslave everyone in it."

"Who is the Black Count?" Walker asked.

"He's like the king," said Eddie, "only he's the King of Darkness. He used to control all of Diabolonia until King Leukos defeated him. Now his power is limited to the Outer Wastes, although our king is convinced that he's getting closer."

"But Lumina thinks he's too weak to be a real threat," Walker said.

"That's what she'd like to think," Eddie assured him. "Lumina was a young warrior in the last war with the Black Count, and during the Battle of Barren Plains something happened to her—nobody knows what and she won't talk about it—but whatever it was it changed her. You may think her hair's white because she's old, but it's been that way ever since then. No, she may not want it to be so, but the threat's real enough, all right. Remember your dream last night, the real scary one? Well, if the Shroud took over it would be like that, only ten times worse."

A shudder ran down Walker's back at the thought of it. Then another shudder ran down his spine when he realized that he had never mentioned a word to Eddie about his dreams.

"How do you know what I dreamed about last night?"

he asked. "I never told you about them."

"I was the one who sent them to you—me and the king," Eddie informed him. "He sent you the nice one with the unicorn and your girlfriend."

"She's *not* my girlfriend," Walker protested. "And you can't send people dreams. They're private."

"If you're desperate you can," Eddie assured him, "and we need you to step up and become King Leukos's heir. The future of the Kingdom depends on it."

"If it's so important, why did the king tell me I only had to be his heir if I wanted to?" Walker replied. "Why couldn't someone else be king? Why couldn't you? You're a prince, so you're halfway there already."

"I may be a prince, but I'm not a Chosen One, and only Chosen Ones can rule," said Eddie. "That's all I can tell you. Come back to the Kingdom, I beg of you."

CHAPTER 8

Astrodor pulled on the gold-edged gown of a page in the royal household. He smoothed it down and looked at himself in the large mirror on the wall. The uniform looked good, he thought, but not as good as the armor of a knight.

"One of these days," he told the mirror, "you'll be looking at His Majesty's Loyal Lightkeeper, the noble Astrodor!"

It was what he wanted more than anything else Nebula could offer. It wouldn't be easy, he knew. It had been hard enough to become a page, and he probably wouldn't be one now if it was not for the fact that his father was a teacher in the Kingdom's only school. Teachers were revered in Nebula and their families were given special privileges, but they were also held to higher standards. So Astrodor worked hard and energetically did everything he was told as fast as he could, although perhaps he should slow down a bit. Running into that new Chosen One in front of the king probably hadn't helped his career.

Astrodor left the dressing area and went into the family room. Houses in the Kingdom only ever had one bedroom, solely for the use of the frail and elderly or the sick. Because of the energy that every citizen got from the Source nobody slept until they became advanced in age, and Astrodor was too young to be tired. He was the eldest child of the family, with three younger brothers, Artor and the twins, Avradin and Amradin, and one sister, Amalia. The twins were the only ones in the family room when Astrodor entered it.

"Where's everyone else?" he asked.

"Mom and Amalia have gone visiting," said Avradin. "I dunno where Dad is."

"Staying out of trouble, I hope," Astrodor said.

"Is he in trouble?" asked Amradin.

"He will be if he keeps telling his students that the king only won the War Against Darkness because he was lucky," Astrodor replied.

"Is that bad?" asked Avradin.

"Bad!" said Astrodor. "It's almost treason. Everyone knows that the king was a hero during that war and that if he hadn't won the Battle of Barren Plains, Nebula would've been overrun by the Shroud."

The twins looked up at him, their eyes wide with fear.

"Will he lose his job and have to work in the stone quarry?" Amradin asked.

"I doubt it," Astrodor reassured them. "Teachers are way too valuable to get rid of. I have to go to the palace. I'll see you at Quiet Hour."

He hugged the twins good-bye and walked down the short garden path and onto the street. Two of his friends, also pages, were waiting for him on the corner of a wide avenue. They usually walked to work together, although Astrodor hardly ever walked anywhere, but sped along half jogging.

"Astrodor, slow down, will you?" one of the friends pleaded.

"You two always take forever," Astrodor protested.

"Come on! We may be missing something at the Palace."

Grumbling, the other two pages tried to keep up with him until they saw something that stopped all three of them dead in their tracks. A juggler was balanced on a board on top of a large ball while tossing several smaller balls high in the air. He was always in the same place and normally the pages paid no attention to him. But today a small boy ran around the corner chased by another boy and a girl. He ran straight into the juggler, knocking the board out from beneath his feet and causing him to come crashing to the ground. The boy ran over to the man to try to help him up.

"I'm sorry, sir," the boy said. "I didn't see you and I was going too fast."

The juggler looked at him and raised his hand as if to strike him.

"Get out of here, you little brat!" he yelled.

"Hey, stop that!" someone in the crowd called back. "Leave him alone. He's just a child."

"He may be just a child," another of the onlookers cried out, "but he should be kept under control! Parents have no idea how to bring up children nowadays!"

A fearsome shouting match broke out with the audience taking sides either with the juggler or with the little boy, who by this time had run away, terrified. The pages stood watching, openmouthed. They had never witnessed people arguing in the street before, and as for striking a child, well, that meant working in the stone quarry for the rest of your life.

The juggler wanted nothing to do with the argument. He picked up his board and balls and walked angrily away. The boys looked at one another.

"Wow!" exclaimed one. "That was scary."

"My dad saw the same sort of thing a couple of cycles ago," said the other. "He'd never seen anything like it either, and he's old. He says that Nebula's changing, and not for the better."

"Let's go before it changes any more," said Astrodor. "I don't want to be late."

Walker looked at Eddie after hearing his plea to return to the Kingdom. His shoulders were hunched in despair, and he looked tired.

"Okay," he finally said. "I'll return to the Kingdom, but on two conditions—that I can come back here whenever I want, and that going there doesn't mean I've decided to be the king's heir."

Eddie thought for a moment.

"All right then, it's agreed."

"On your honor?" asked Walker.

"Everything I do is on my honor," Eddie replied pompously.

"Oh," Walker added, "and that Frankie comes with us."

"That's three conditions," Eddie pointed out, "and the answer is no."

"Why not?" Walker protested.

"I can't go bringing every Tom, Dick, or Harriet to the Kingdom!" Eddie cried. "We'd end up with half the Outerworld, and there's just not that much room."

"It's not half the Outerworld," Walker protested. "It's only one skinny girl."

"No," said Eddie.

"If she doesn't go, I don't go," said Walker determinedly, crossing his arms as he spoke.

"Oh for goodness' sake!" cried Eddie in exasperation. "You're the most stubborn person I've met for centuries. Well, if you're really determined then I suppose we'll have to take her, although I'm still against it. I know things have changed since I was born, but in my experience girls are no use when it comes to defending Kingdoms."

"I bet she would be," Walker said, "but that's not why

I want her along. I just want someone from the Outer-world with me while I make up my mind."

"All right, all right," Eddie said. "I agree. Let's go get her."

"I don't even know if she's home," Walker said.

"She's home," Eddie assured him.

"How do you know?" asked Walker

"I just know," Eddie replied. "Let's go. I'll beat you there."

Eddie started running down the dirt road toward Frankie's house, even though Walker had never told him where she lived. He was surprised at how fast Eddie moved, especially since he was carrying his heavy sword. It was almost as if his feet never touched the ground.

By the time they got to Frankie's front door Walker was panting, but Eddie didn't seem to be breathing any faster. Walker grabbed hold of the black metal door-knocker and rapped sharply. After a few minutes the door swung open to reveal a very tall, very thin woman with a tired and worried expression on her face.

"Yes?" was all she said.

"Please, can Frankie come out?" Walker asked.

"Oh, you must be the boy from down the road—the Watson child," the woman said. "Let me see what she's doing." She closed the door, leaving them standing on the step.

"She needs feeding up, that one," Eddie declared.

Walker looked at his strange companion with his shoulder-length red hair, his fedora, and his sword.

"Don't you think you should hide, maybe?" he asked. "Frankie's mom may not want her going around with weird people."

"Weird yourself," Eddie retorted. "What's weird about me? Anyway, she can't see me or hear me, so even if I *was* weird it wouldn't make any difference."

Then the door flew open and Frankie burst out, almost knocking him over. Today's T-shirt said HIGH MAINTENANCE BUT WORTH IT.

"You came to my house!" she enthused. "How cool. That means we really are friends. Maybe we should cut ourselves and exchange blood to make it official. It wouldn't have to be a big cut, just a little nick, really."

Walker didn't think that was a good idea at all, so he changed the subject.

"Eddie says he'll take you to the Kingdom," he said.

"Yay!" She screamed with delight. "Excellent. When do we go? When do I meet him? Oh, this is soooo great!"

"He's right there," said Walker, pointing to Eddie, who was glowering with disapproval.

"Where?" asked Frankie, looking in the direction that Walker was pointing.

"Eddie, please stop that," Walker pleaded. "How can you take her to the Kingdom if she can't see or hear you?"

"I've changed my mind," said Eddie.

"Well, I haven't," Walker assured him. "So if you'd just go away please and leave us alone, we have things to do."

Frankie looked quite bewildered, but not nearly as confused as she did when she suddenly saw Eddie standing right next to her.

"All right, then. If that's the way you're going to be," said Eddie, "we'll all go."

"Oh wow!" cried Frankie. "How d'you do that? That *is* amazing! I'm Frankie, by the way."

"No kidding!" said Eddie. "I kinda guessed that. You're the only skinny girl around here that I can see."

"And I'm kinda guessing that you're rude, and it's not cool to be rude to people you just met," said Frankie.

"Oh, I'm so sorry." Eddie smirked. "If I upset you that much maybe you'd prefer to stay here and not have to be in my company."

"Nice try, buster," said Frankie, "but I don't upset easily."

"Will you two stop?" yelled Walker. "You're making me remember why I never wanted friends."

Much to Walker's surprise they both fell silent.

"Are we going to the Kingdom or not?" he demanded.

"Yes," grumbled Eddie. "We're going."

The three of them made their way back to the hole in the ground and stood on its edge.

"Now hold hands and don't let go until we're in motion," Eddie said sternly.

"How will we know we're in motion?" asked Frankie.

"You'll know because you're moving," replied Eddie. "That's what motion means."

"Is he always this nasty?" Frankie asked Walker.

Walker just sighed, shrugged his shoulders, and took hold of her hand. He felt Eddie's hand close around his other one.

"On the count of three we jump," Eddie commanded. "One—two—three!"

They leaped into the air, and instead of the jarring sensation on their feet and ankles, they were enveloped in the smooth, silky blackness and strange floating feeling that Walker now knew meant they were on their way to the Kingdom. After what seemed both forever and no time at all they found themselves standing upright, only this time they were in the courtyard of the Palace.

"Oh—my—God!" Frankie cried. "That was totally awesome—I mean absolutely, completely the most amazing thing that ever happened to me, way better than snowboarding."

She looked around in wonder, staring at the people, the buildings, and the silver birds high above her head.

"This," she said in an unusually hushed voice, "is the most beautiful place I've seen anywhere."

Walker looked at her with admiration; she seemed to have no fear. He also noticed for the first time how pretty she was. She glowed, not just in the way that everybody in the Kingdom glowed, but also because of excitement and anticipation. Then anxiety overtook him. He knew that by coming back he could be walking into a trap. Even though the king had let him return to the Outerworld before, there was no guarantee he would again, and bad as it would be to be captive himself, it would be far worse to know that Frankie was caged because of him.

CHAPTER 9

Walker was still a little anxious as they mounted the steps to the Royal Apartments. But he also found he was feeling surprisingly at home. It was fun to be here with Frankie. He was wary of strange things himself, but all the way to the castle she had been exclaiming with wonder and delight.

"Look at that cute dragon!"

"Wow, what a weird instrument! How great would it be to have one of those in our school band?"

"Look at that tightrope walker. I'd *love* to walk a tight-rope."

These and many more things in the Kingdom capti-vated Frankie, who didn't seem to be the least bit worried about being in a strange world from which there was no guarantee of return. As they climbed the stairs Walker could hear her continuing commentary on everything they saw.

Luzaro met them in the hallway outside the ante-chamber.

"Welcome back, Your Highness, my lord," he said, nodding to both the boys, "and welcome to you, Miss Frankie, as well."

"How does he know my name?" whispered Frankie to Walker.

"They seem to know everything," he answered.

"Oooh, how spooky," said Frankie. "Even that I'm wearing the same socks as yesterday?"

"Probably," Walker replied.

"Yikes," Frankie said. "I'm not sure I could live here."

Then, as if to disprove all Walker had just told her, Fussingham came bursting through the curtain.

"Just one moment, just one moment!" he cried. "I have no record of this young woman. What is your name, child? I need details."

"Frankie," replied Frankie, without missing a beat. "Actually Frances Livonia Hayes, but you can call me Frankie. Put down I was born in Mass General, you must know it, it's that huge hospital, you can't miss it, and both my parents are lawyers, although actually my dad will probably be a judge soon, but my mom does real estate, and while she says it's much more boring than criminal—that's what my dad does right now—she also makes much more money, in fact heaps of it, and although she'll never be on the Supreme Court, which my dad could be although it's unlikely, she's the one that paid for the house down the road from Walker, which is how I met him and how I came to be here."

Fussingham's silver feather pen was scratching furiously over the pages of the book he carried wherever he went. She looked over his shoulder.

"No," she said. "'Judge' is spelled *j-u-D-g-e*."

"Maybe, Fussingham," said Luzaro impatiently, "you could get this down later. The king wishes to see these three young people."

"Yes, quite," replied Fussingham. "Later. Good idea."

For the time being he was a beaten man.

Luzaro led them into the antechamber, which was

empty of Lightkeepers or anyone else, and had a desolate look about it, as did the king. He was sprawled on his throne at the far end, and seemed distracted and tired.

"Come here, come here." He beckoned them over. "I am glad to see you return, Chosen One. I understand that we cannot yet hope for you as our future king, but the fact that you are here once more is encouragement enough at a time when there is little else to find reassuring. Luzaro said this young lady persuaded you to come back, and for that we thank her."

"I don't know how much persuading I did, King," she said with unusual modesty, "but I'm glad I did. You have a very cool Kingdom."

"Ah, well, indeed there are chill winds blowing closer every day," said the king, completely misunderstanding her. "It is most troubling."

Luzaro appeared at the curtain once more.

"The Lightkeepers have returned, Your Majesty," he announced.

"Bring them in, Luzaro. Bring them in."

The king turned back to the three children.

"Our situation gets graver by the moment, although I am the only one who seems to see it," he said, "and I have much to decide with my counselors. Go with my page until I have finished with them. I must talk more with you, Chosen One, about whether or not you wish to be king."

He sat up and yelled, "Page!" at the top of his voice. From the far end of the room Astrodor pushed open the curtain and hurried toward the throne.

"Page, take these young people with you and entertain them while I am with my Lightkeepers. Bring the Chosen One back to me just before the next Quiet Hour."

Astrodor led the three friends out of the antechamber as the Lightkeepers filed in. Their faces were grim, and Walker was glad to be away from the heavy feeling that hung over them. When they got into the courtyard everything felt lighter and more cheerful, the way it had seemed when he first arrived there.

"What would you like to do?" asked Astrodor.

"I don't know," Walker replied. "What is there?"

"We could go to the quarry and watch them mining the stone," Eddie suggested. "That's always interesting."

"Or we could go to the unicorn farm and watch the babies being trained," added Astrodor.

"Baby unicorns get my vote!" cried Frankie. "I mean, how cute can a block of stone be?"

"That would be great," Walker agreed, "but there's

something else I'd like to do—go to Astrodor's house."

"My house?" said Astrodor. "There's nothing special about my house or my family. We're just ordinary Nebulites. Why would you want to go there?"

"It's because you're ordinary people, it would be interesting," Walker explained. "We've spent a lot of time with the king and all the Lightkeepers but not with just regular folks."

Frankie looked at him curiously.

"You know, you're right," she said. "It would be kind of fun. I love seeing inside other people's houses, 'specially if they're messy. We can go to the farm afterward."

"Let's do it," Walker said, "but only if your family wouldn't mind, of course."

"I'm sure they would be honored to have a Chosen One in their house," Astrodor assured him. "I don't know who's at home right now."

"Well," said Frankie, "there's only one way to find out. Let's go!"

And so they followed their new friend along the same streets he had walked on his way to work. Walker could feel a tension in the air that hadn't been there on his first visit. Not every face was smiling. He overheard snatches of muttered conversation: ". . . think they're better than

87

we are . . ." and ". . . just an Outerworld boy . . ." It was all very disturbing. Finally Astrodor stopped in front of his home.

"Like I said," he mumbled, "it's nothing special. It's just like everybody else's house."

"That's great," said Frankie. "That means we don't have to go into any others. You've seen one—you've seen them all!"

They filed down the short garden path and through the open entryway that led straight into the main room. Lying on the floor were the twins, Avradin and Amradin. They were playing with small stone bricks that interlocked, and were halfway through building what looked to Walker like a fort. Behind them sat Artor on a very uncomfortable-looking stone chair reading a large book, the pages of which appeared to be made of fabric. They all looked up as their brother and the three strangers entered the room.

"Hello, my brothers," Astrodor greeted them. "I want you to meet some people."

The twins looked curiously at the visitors, but Artor buried himself deeper into his book.

"This is Prince Edward," Astrodor continued. "He's a Royal Messenger and you may have seen him before.

He's the king's messenger and one of the most important people in court."

Eddie looked both pleased and embarrassed by this description, and muttered something about that being a bit of an exaggeration.

"And I'm Frankie," said Frankie, who never needed anyone else to introduce her. "I'm from the Outerworld, which is a long way from here—at least I think it is! And this is Walker," she continued. "He's from the Outerworld too. We live near each other."

"Actually this is Lord Walker," Astrodor corrected her. "He's a Chosen One."

Amradin looked up from his building blocks, suddenly interested in the visitors for the first time.

"Are you going to be king one day?" he asked Walker.

"Can we see the mark?" his brother Avradin chimed in.

They gathered around Walker, staring at his cheek as if it was the most amazing thing they had ever seen.

"You know, being with you is like being with a celebrity," Frankie observed.

Fame was the last thing that Walker wanted. He had always tried to go unnoticed.

"It's just something that happened when I was born," he protested. "It's not like I did anything good to get it.

It could have happened to anyone."

"No, no, my lord," said Astrodor, "the mark is only given to those of outstanding character. It says so in our history books."

Eddie let out a sound that was halfway between a sigh and a growl. He was getting as tired of the Walker admiration as Walker was himself.

"Let's do something fun," he said. "How about a game of rocks?"

This had the effect of taking the attention away from Walker, much to his relief. The twins disappeared into their room and returned a few moments later with a fabric bag full of round stones. They drew a circle in the dust on the floor and dropped most of them into the middle, reserving six for each player. The object of the game was to knock as many of your opponents' rocks out of the circle, much like marbles, and each time one was hit a cloud of dust rose into the air. Walker had only ever played card games by himself or sometimes with his mother, but soon he was on his knees with the other children and yelling as loud as they did when one of his rocks struck an opponent's.

It seemed there were two competitions taking place: one to win the contest, the other to see who could make the most noise. Because of this nobody heard Astrodor's mother and father enter the room along with the boys' sister, Amalia. It was only the strange doglike creature that came in with them that took the boys' attention away from their game. Artor suddenly put his book down and whistled to the animal that looked as if it was made of shiny steel wool.

"Arv—come here, boy," he said, and then, as an after-thought, "Hi, Mom; hi, Dad."

The boys' father stood there with a stern look on his face.

"What exactly," he asked, "is going on here?"

"Father," Astrodor addressed him respectfully, "the king asked me to take care of these children for a while, and they said they wanted to see a normal Nebulite home, so I brought them here to visit. Two of them come from the Outerworld, you see."

"I'm perfectly well aware of who they are and where they come from," his father assured him gruffly, "and I'm also well aware," he continued, looking at Eddie, "who this person is and what his reputation is."

"My dear, please, show a little respect," said their mother. "This young man is a Chosen One, after all."

"Oh, a Chosen One! So what makes him different?

Nothing more than a mark on his skin, that's all," said the father. "I don't know who chose him, but it wasn't me."

"We're happy to have you visit. It's an honor to have a Chosen One among us," the mother said.

"He's a child," said the father. "He's just a child, no better than our own. All this Chosen One nonsense—it's just an old superstition."

And with that he went into one of the rooms in the back of the house, leaving Walker perplexed.

"Wow!" Frankie whispered in his ear. "I'm glad he's not my teacher. I'd have to change schools."

"I'm sorry," Walker apologized to Astrodor's mother. "We didn't mean to cause trouble. We just wanted to come over and play."

"Don't take any notice of my husband," she assured him. "He has some funny ideas. Where he gets them from I'm sure I don't know."

Suddenly Artor stopped stroking his pet and tilted his head to one side.

"Rider headed this way," he said.

Everyone else listened, but none of them could hear anything.

"Artor's senses are unusually acute," said his mother.

And sure enough, moments later Jevon appeared in the doorway.

"Jevon," Eddie said, "what's up? Why are you here?"

"His Majesty requests a meeting with the Chosen One immediately. It is of high importance and I have been sent here to fetch him," the knight replied.

"Just the Chosen One, not me?" Eddie asked anxiously.

"Just the Chosen One," Jevon replied.

"Not me either," Frankie pointed out to Eddie. "So we'll just hang here with Astrodor. Walker'll come back soon enough."

Walker could see that Eddie was upset about being left out.

"You know, Eddie," he said, "if seeing the king is urgent it probably means bad news. As soon as I've seen him I'll come straight back here and let you know what happened."

"I know. You're right," said Eddie. "I just wish he trusted me more than he does."

Walker turned toward the knight.

"Okay," he said, "I'm ready to go."

CHAPTER 10

The unicorn galloped down the streets toward the palace. Whenever anything got in the way it leaped into the air, flying over every obstacle without slackening its pace. Walker was seated on the unicorn's back behind Jevon. The steady drum of hooves was interrupted by moments of quiet as the animal flew over the next hurdle. When that happened all Walker could hear was the whistling of the air as it sped past his ears.

As they galloped into the Palace courtyard another

page was waiting for them and he quickly took the creature's reins. Jevon leaped from the saddle in one swift motion and then lifted Walker down.

"Come," he said, "we must make haste."

They hurried up the stairs. The Palace was eerily empty. Even Luzaro and Fussingham were nowhere to be seen. When they entered the antechamber they saw the king standing alone looking out one of the windows. He beckoned them toward him.

"Thank you, Jevon, for your speed," he said. "Now please leave us and rally whatever Lightkeepers you can to accompany us, although I fear it will be very few."

"I will do my best, sire," Jevon replied.

Bowing as he went, the knight left the room.

"He is a brave and honorable man," the king said to Walker. "If I had more like him I would breathe easier. Come here, young man, sit by me, and let me tell you what is about to happen."

He walked toward one of the stone benches that lined the room, and indicated Walker should follow him. When they were seated he turned toward Walker and took both his hands.

"Now listen to me carefully," he said, looking intently at Walker's face. "This is important. We sent another patrol to make contact with Litherium, and they too failed to get through, only this time they were not just turned back by fierce winds; they were destroyed by the power of the Black Shroud. The only survivor was a young page who accompanied them. How he escaped we do not know. Neither do we know the fate of the citizens of Litherium. The patrol was attacked before it reached them but I suspect the news isn't good."

Walker sat still and silent. What the king said was frightening, and Walker didn't know why Leukos was telling him. What could he do? The king got up and led them both back to the window he had been looking through when they entered. As Walker gazed out he saw the city sparkling in front of him, its crowded streets pulsing with life.

"I have ruled these people longer than you can imagine," the king continued, "and I love them dearly. They are good people, not every one, and not all the time, but they are worthy of my protection, and that I will give them until the last breath in my body. I intend to lead those of the Lightkeepers who will accompany me out to Litherium, and, if that has fallen, even beyond, until I can find a Sister City able to join us and fight the Black Count once again."

"But why do you think you'll be able to do what the other patrols couldn't?" Walker asked.

"We will be armed with Lances of Light," the king replied. "Do you recall the spears that hung around the walls of the Sanctuary where the Source resides? They have been there since the last battle with the Shroud, and they were the weapons that helped us defeat them. During the many Eons since then they have been absorbing energy from the sphere, and they can emit a powerful light that is like a deadly poison to our enemies."

"Why didn't the patrols use them?" Walker asked.

"The lances are powerful," the king explained, "but they take a long time to absorb that power, and when they are spent they are useless, so we only use them in times of extreme urgency."

"Why don't you just order all the Lightkeepers to come with you?" Walker asked. "After all, you are the king."

"A knight who doesn't passionately believe in the cause for which you're fighting is worse than useless," the king replied. "No, give me a few good men or women who will be with me to the end, whatever that may be, and I will take them over legions of the halfhearted."

"Why are you telling me this?" asked Walker. This was the question that had been in his mind from the beginning, but that he had been afraid to ask.

"You may think that the mark you bear upon your cheek was an accident of birth," the king said, "and I suppose it was, in the same way that courage is an accident of birth, or honesty, or virtue. But I can tell you that the mark is only given to those who have all of these qualities and others besides. Had you been born in our world as my son you would have been my worthy successor. However, you are not of this world, and your fate is elsewhere. I am not asking you to be my heir, but what I am asking, even begging you, is that you will remain here until my mission is over, and if it ends badly that you will use the strengths that you possess to guide my people until they find a worthy leader to replace you."

To Walker this didn't sound like such a good deal. It seemed you got the bad parts of being king without any of the good. But even though he had only known the king a short time there was something about this old man that he admired. He never seemed worried about himself, and only thought of what was best for his people. Walker had never been quite sure what made a good person, but he felt that the king was one.

There was, of course, always the possibility that Leukos would be successful, and defeat the Black Shroud. Then everything in the Kingdom would go back to normal, and Walker would be released of the burden the king was asking him to accept. He thought for a moment, trying to make up his mind. He finally decided.

"Okay," he said, "I'll do it, but on three conditions."

"And what would they be?" the king asked curiously.

"That you teach me how to go between the Kingdom and the Outerworld by myself," Walker replied. "That way I won't feel trapped here and I can see my mom and dad whenever I want to. And I also want you to teach me how to make people forget they've seen me like Eddie can do. Oh, and I would like to have my own unicorn."

The king laughed, his face creasing into a thousand lines.

"You are a tough negotiator!" he said. "So, let's see. The first one is easy—for you, at least. Impossible for me because only people with Outerworld blood in their veins can journey between the two worlds. The secret is to picture in your mind's eye exactly where you want to end up. Then you run as fast as you can, thinking only about your destination. Do not think about anything else, and in the blink of a dragon's eye you'll be there. The unicorn is not a problem. I'll send orders to the Mistress of the Herd to pick out a nice one for you. As for the forgetting part, that's trickier. You may have to wait until my return for that one."

There was a movement at the far end of the room, and Jevon appeared, his face set in a grim expression.

"I have the knights assembled, sire," he said, "ready for you to lead them to Litherium."

"How many will be in our number?" asked the king.

"Apart from me, sire, there are six," Jevon replied.

"Six!" exploded the king. "Out of all that band of brave warriors, only six will go with me to our Sister City? Why so?"

"The others claim to have more important things to do and beg to be excused," Jevon said.

"Ah," said the king. "Of course. More important things like jousting and playing infernally bad music and tossing balls in the air. Much more important than saving the Kingdom or our cousins in Litherium."

He sighed a deep sigh.

"Oh well," he said. "So be it. Who will fight with us?"

"They are your most experienced Lightkeepers, my king," Jevon assured him.

"Experienced! Oh dear!" exclaimed the king. "You mean old. Only the old will join me, because only they have any memory of the Shroud."

"Their skills will compensate for their age, sire," Jevon said.

"Let's hope so," said the king. "I will go to the Sanctuary and get seven lances."

"Unless you don't intend to carry one yourself, sire," Jevon corrected him, "you will need eight. There are seven in our party if you include me."

"I don't include you, Jevon," said the king. "I need you here in case we don't return. You are the only one I trust to help this young man. He has the wisdom of the mark, but he is yet a boy, and hasn't the strength of a grown man. You must be that part of him."

Jevon looked crestfallen. Then he bowed before the king.

"I have taken a sacred oath of loyalty to you, Your Majesty," he said, "and I will do as you instruct even though my heart is elsewhere."

"I know you will," said the king. Then he shouted for a page and the boy who had taken the unicorn's reins appeared once more.

"Accompany this young lord to his destination, and tell the Mistress of the Herd to provide him with one of her best unicorns. We cannot have a Chosen One depending on the charity of others for his rides."

He turned to Walker, took his hands, and looked him straight in the eyes with such sorrow that the boy feared he was about to cry.

"I hope to return," he said, "because, old as I am, I would like to live a little longer, but also because I would like to have the time to know you better. You are a fine young man, and I would like to watch you grow into the person you are destined to become."

Then he turned and strode out of the room, closely followed by Jevon.

"Where do you wish to go, my lord?" the page asked.

"Back to Astrodor's," Walker replied. "It's okay, you don't have to show me. I can find my way."

When Walker got back to the house, things were pretty much as he had left them. Eddie was on the floor with the twins, only now, instead of playing rocks, they were erecting a tall tower from the building stones. Artor was still reading and Astrodor and Frankie were sitting together in a corner talking. There was no sign of either parent. When they saw Walker return they clamored around him, asking what had happened, and had he agreed to be the king's heir, and would he be going back to the Outerworld ever again.

"I will be going back to the Outerworld often," he told them, "and by myself."

This brought a gasp from the listeners.

"So he taught you how to do that, did he?" Eddie asked somewhat sullenly. "Well, let me tell you, it's not as easy as you would think."

"When you say you're going back by yourself," Frankie questioned him, "do you mean alone or just without help? Because if you're going I'm coming with you, so don't think I'm not."

"Okay, then. Are you ready now?" Walker asked, grasping her hand.

"You're leaving me here?" Eddie was incredulous. "I mean, just like that?"

"I've got to try this," Walker said. "Otherwise I can't stay here. If we don't return straight away come find us. It'll mean I don't know how to get us back."

"I just hope you get there," Eddie warned him, "and don't get stuck somewhere between the two worlds. It would be tricky to rescue you if that happened."

"It's a risk I'm going to take," said Walker. "How about you?" he asked Frankie.

"Hey," she replied. "You're a Chosen One. How bad could it be?"

They said good-bye to everyone and walked out of the house and down the street toward the avenue that ran from the Palace to the gates. When they got to the wider road Walker gripped Frankie's hand tightly and they started to run. He closed his eyes and thought of the orchard behind the barn. Faster and faster they ran, quicker than Walker had ever run before. Suddenly there was a crash and a blow that knocked the wind out of him. He looked around to see that he had run directly into the side of the barn. Sprawled in front of him was Frankie, covered in mud and grass. Behind her he could see the sun shining through the leaves of the apple trees. She looked up at him.

"Eddie's right, you know," she gasped. "This stuff is harder than it looks."

CHAPTER 11

E ddie watched Walker and Frankie go down the path toward the street. He wondered what he should do while they were away. He could follow them back to the Outerworld but that would be as good as admitting that he was jealous and felt left out, and there was no way he was going to do that.

He said good-bye to the boys and walked aimlessly toward the big avenue. Then he noticed that a crowd had gathered and was lining the sides of the avenue. He gently pushed his way to the front and saw the king and six of his Lightkeepers on unicorns some distance from him. He knew it was the king because someone mounted on a jet-black steed led the group, and the sovereign was the only one to have such a unicorn; every other one in the Kingdom was white. The story went that the animal, Tonar, once belonged to the Black Count, but during the Battle of Barren Plains it threw him from its back and ran to the king when his mount was killed during the fighting. They had been inseparable ever since.

As the royal party got closer Eddie could see that the knights held Lances of Light. He wondered why there were so few riders and why they were all so old. He turned to one of the onlookers.

"What's happening, do you know?" he asked.

"From what I hear," replied the man, "they're going to try to get through to Litherium again, although why they think they can do it when other patrols have failed I don't know. Still, he's the king so he probably has information we don't."

"Don't you believe it," said a voice behind them. "I think he's gotten too old for the job. He's going senile. We need new leaders, in my opinion."

Eddie whirled around to see who was speaking. You

never heard anyone criticizing the king; it was unthinkable. Everyone else seemed as disturbed as he was, but nobody could tell who had made the remark. He moved to the back of the throng and walked in the same direction as the riders—toward the huge gates in the wall. The crowd thickened as he got closer, and he had to push his way through.

A plan had formed in his mind. He would try and slip through the gates when they were opened to let the king and his party out. Then if he hung behind until it was too late for them to send him back, he would join the group and go to Litherium. It was many Eons since he'd been to a Sister City. Not only would it be exciting, but it would also show Walker and Frankie that he could live without them. He might not be a Chosen One, but he was still a prince of the realm and important in his own right.

The riders were now in front of the gates. They halted and the huge doors began to slowly open. Eddie noticed that as they did, a gap appeared under one of the massive hinges. It wasn't big, but big enough for an eleven-year-old to slip through.

"Look at the power of those lances," he said in a voice loud enough for everyone around him to hear. The surrounding crowd turned their heads to see what he was talking about, and as they did he slipped through the gap and into the vast darkness beyond the walls.

"We have to go back," said Walker.

"Why?" asked Frankie, who was lying in the orchard idly chewing on a blade of grass. "We just got here."

"I promised the king I would stay in Nebula until he returned," Walker explained. "I only wanted to come here to see if I could."

"You just want to get back to see if they've got that unicorn thing ready for you," Frankie suggested. "But if you're going to be all antsy, let's go now. We don't even know if it'll work from this side. We might have to wait until Eddie comes to get us. Think how happy he'll be if that happens."

Walker was worried about the return journey too. The king had only described the process from the Kingdom to the Outerworld. Walker assumed it would work the same in reverse, but there was only one way to find out.

"We need more open space than we have here to get up enough speed," he said. "Let's go to the meadow."

Next to the orchard there was a cow field with plenty of room for them to run without banging into anything. Walker took Frankie's hand and the two of them began to sprint across the grass. He concentrated with all his might on the square in the middle of the Palace. They kept going and going but nothing changed. He finally brought them to a halt.

"Nothing happened," he said.

"Oh, yes it did!" cried Frankie. "Yuck. Look at my shoes. How gross!"

He looked down to see her sneakers covered in cow manure and grinned.

"Well, you're a real country girl now," he said.

"I smell like one," she replied. "What's more, we're still here."

Walker banged his forehead with the palm of his hand.

"Of course! We have to use the hole from this side!" he cried. "That was so stupid!"

"It would have been nice if you'd remembered that before I got covered in all this poop," she complained.

They went back through the fence and over to the hole behind the barn. Standing on the edge, Walker once again concentrated on the square. He held Frankie's hand.

"Jump on three," he told her. "One—two—three!"

They leaped into the air and were immediately enveloped in the sensation of floating in space. He landed in the middle of the square and looked around to find Frankie. There was a loud splash and he turned to see her standing ankle-deep in the water of the fountain. She looked at him crossly.

"Next time," she said as she climbed out, "I think I'll wait for Eddie."

"Well, at least your shoes are clean now," he said. Fortunately Astrodor found them before Walker could get himself into any more trouble.

"Did Prince Edward come back with you?" he inquired.

"Back?" Walker replied. "He didn't even come with us."

"Really?" said Astrodor. "He followed you out and I just assumed he was going along."

"Nope," said Frankie. "We didn't see him at all."

"Oh well," Astrodor said, "I expect he's around somewhere. It must be so amazing to go to the Outerworld and come back whenever you want to. Was it easy?"

"Oh, yeah, it was no problem," Walker assured him. Then, looking at Frankie's soaking socks and shoes, he added, "Well, nothing major, anyway."

"That's great," said Astrodor. "Oh, I forgot, Lord Jevon told me he promised the king to take you to the unicorn farm to get a mount."

"When did the king leave?" Walker asked.

"About two cycles ago," Astrodor replied. "We've heard nothing from them up to now. Anyway, when do you want to go to the farm? The Mistress of the Herd said she has a really great one picked out for you. You are so lucky you're getting a unicorn of your very own right now. I probably won't get one until I'm a Lightkeeper and that could be Eons away. When would you like to see it?"

"Let's do it now," said Frankie, "before he explodes with excitement."

Walker didn't even bother to deny his eagerness, and so they all made their way to the unicorn farm. It was a long walk, near the rock quarry and far away from the settlements. It wasn't big but Walker could make out pens containing forty to fifty unicorns, all of different ages and sizes. He and Frankie were stroking a group of foals and letting them nibble their fingers when a stern-looking woman strode up. Instead of the normal floor-length gown she wore white baggy pants and high boots.

"You must be the Chosen One here to claim his mount," she said to Walker. "My name is Amula. I'm the Mistress of the Herd and I have her waiting for you. Come, follow me."

She turned on her heels and headed toward the buildings at one end of the pens. *No wonder the unicorns are well trained,* Walker thought as he trotted after her.

As they turned the corner on the largest building he stopped and gasped. There before him, tethered to a ring in the wall, stood an animal that was so beautiful he just had to stare at her. She was not the largest in the herd, but what she lacked in size she made up for in elegance. Her tail reached to the ground, and her mane was long and wavy. A thick forelock brushed the edges of her eyes, and her coat was a light creamy color but was flecked with pure silver that made it sparkle.

"Wow," said Frankie. "I'm no unicorn expert but that is one good-looking beast."

Walker went up to her and stroked her nose. She nuzzled him affectionately. Her eyes were bright green, just like Eddie's, and they shone with the same intensity. Protruding from the center of her forehead was a stubby horn. Amula saw him touch it.

"She's young, but it will grow in," she assured him.

"What's her name?" he almost whispered.

"Doesn't have one," said Amula. "We always let the knights name them."

"But I'm not a knight," Walker pointed out.

"If you have one of the king's unicorns you are," Amula declared. "Choose a name."

Walker thought for a minute.

"I'm going to call her Lightning," he decided.

Amula had clearly never heard of lightning, because she shrugged her shoulders and said: "Strange name, but Lightning it is, then. Let me get a saddle and bridle. I'll get a double saddle. I presume the young lady will be riding behind you, and we don't want her falling off."

She said it in a tone of voice that indicated she didn't care either way, and walked off.

"What did I do to upset her?" Frankie asked.

"I dunno," said Walker. "Maybe she just likes animals better than people."

"Well, I like animals better than her, especially this one," she said as she stroked Lightning's nose. "She's beautiful."

Lightning let out a long, low whinny and gently pressed her head against Frankie's chest. Frankie was clearly in love. Amula returned with a saddle that had two seats in it, one for each rider, and two sets of stirrups. The bridle was simply a band that went over the nose, with long reins attached. Amula fitted them on the unicorn and handed the reins to Walker.

"What do I do?" he asked.

"Tell her that you want to mount," she instructed.

"Okay," Walker said. "I WANT TO MOUNT!"

"There's no need to shout," said Amula. "Her hearing is much more sensitive than yours."

And indeed Lightning was now down on her front knees, bringing the saddle low enough for both of them to hop up. When they were on she rose to her feet again.

"What do I do now?" asked Walker, grabbing the reins tightly.

"The first thing is to relax," said Amula. "Then simply picture in your mind where you want to go and she'll take you there."

"Just like that?" he asked.

"Just like that," she assured him. "Try it out. Go around the back of the farm."

There was a rock-strewn path around the perimeter of the unicorn enclosures, and Walker looked at the farthest point of it he could see. Lightning moved quickly forward, her gait so smooth that her two riders barely felt any movement. As Walker looked farther on, Lightning moved in the same direction.

"Imagine going faster," Frankie whispered in his ear.

He did so and immediately Lightning's pace increased.

"No, faster," urged Frankie.

"Let's go, Lightning," Walker said. "Show us what you've got!"

The unicorn sprang into action and within moments they were racing. Even though they could hear the sound of her hooves on the rough ground, it felt as if they really were soaring through the air. They were on the outer fringes of the Kingdom now, close to the walls, and Lightning was going as fast as she knew how.

The path veered to the right and suddenly Walker could see that their way was blocked by a fall of stones from the side of a round turret. The pens of the farm closed off the other side of the path and there was nowhere for them to go. Before he could think they were on top of the fallen stones. He shut his eyes, and Frankie let out a little "Uh-oh" and tightened her grip around his waist. Then they felt the animal jump, clearing the barrier by several feet. She flew through the air, then landed and smoothly continued on her way. Walker had the good sense to imagine her going slower and within a short time they were back to a gentle walk.

"Wow!" cried Frankie. "Double wow! I don't know what Eddie's doing right now, but I bet it's nowhere near as exciting as this."

CHAPTER 12

E ddie knew from the very beginning that this was a foolish thing to do. The fact that the knights were carrying Lances of Light was a sure indication that the mission was going to be difficult and dangerous. But he did it anyway.

He'd managed to conceal himself for a while, but it was hard to hide his glow, even behind big rocks. It wasn't so much of a problem near to the Kingdom because of the light that spilled from its walls, but the farther they went the darker it became. And the party went farther into Diabolonia than Eddie had ever been. The king had decided that instead of taking the direct road from Nebula to Litherium, they would sweep in a wide circle and approach the Sister City from a completely different direction. If the Warriors of the Black Shroud had captured the city, this would take them by surprise.

Everything started to go wrong when the group stopped to rest. The knights had formed a defensive circle, and the rider facing Eddie saw his glow and immediately went to investigate.

"Your royal highness," said the knight when he discovered him, "this is not a good place for anyone to be, least of all a child. The king will not be pleased."

And indeed the king was far from pleased.

"What in the name of Light possessed you to follow us out here?" he asked sternly. "Didn't you realize you would make a difficult task even harder? Your welfare is now our burden."

Eddie felt foolish and ashamed.

"Please, sire, I wanted to visit Litherium again. It's been a long time since I was there," was all he could think to say.

"You wanted to see Litherium!" the king repeated. "Did you think this was some pleasure trip we were embarked upon? That we were visiting cousins? Don't you realize it is likely the Shroud have already destroyed that city, and that we may happen upon them at any moment?"

He looked down at the small boy, who seemed even smaller next to his huge unicorn.

"Prince Edward," he said in a softer voice, "I know that the curse you have carried for so long hangs heavy upon you, but it will not be lifted through foolish and reckless actions such as this."

Eddie hung his head in shame. He knew that the king spoke the truth.

"Here," said the king, leaning down and offering his hand, "hop up here. There's no point in you skulking around behind rocks for the rest of the mission."

The sovereign grasped Eddie's hand. The older man's grip was strong and he easily lifted him onto the animal's back.

"Hang on," Leukos said, "and put your arms around me. We don't want you falling off. You've been enough trouble already."

They had only been traveling a short time when the temperature plummeted, and Eddie was colder than he had ever been in his life. Then the winds started up, and soon they were howling around the riders. Tonar put his head down and plodded on, his long mane and forelock flying crazily in the wind. The king had leaned forward, pressing his face and body against the beast's neck so that Tonar protected him from the wind, and provided the warmth of his body.

Eddie, too, lay as flat as he could, and glancing behind him he saw that all the other knights were in the same position. They carried their lances low, lighting up the ground in front of their mounts. Slowly the party inched forward. The winds were so strong that even these massive war unicorns could only make sluggish progress. The closer to Litherium they got, the worse the conditions became.

Then he heard a noise like thunder. At first it sounded like any storm in the Outerworld, rumbling in the distance. Suddenly it began to come toward them. It was as if it had seen them and was bearing down directly on them in a straight line. The nearer it got, the louder it became, until they were surrounded by crashes that shook the ground, their mounts, and their very bodies. Once it had located them it swirled around in a whirlpool of fury.

The king shouted orders for the knights to reassemble

into a defensive circle, but none of them could make out what he was saying. Even Eddie, who was seated right behind him, could barely hear his commands. The unicorns were terrified. Although they were bred and trained for battle, none of them except Tonar had experienced anything like it, and it had been many Eons since he had been exposed to such ferocity.

Just when Eddie thought it could get no worse, the ground began to tremble. Thumping sounds could be heard coming toward them, and with each thud the earth shuddered. The knights raised their Lances of Light to illuminate the scene before them, but the winds were so strong they could barely hold them upright.

One of the riders reached into his saddlebag and pulled out a slingshot. He inserted a shining sphere into the sling, raised, and fired it. The shot was powerful and it curved high into the air despite the high winds, and what it lit up was a nightmare.

Lines of monstrous giants faced them, huge creatures dressed entirely in black cloaks, with hoods draped over their faceless heads. It looked as if their skulls were made of a dull metal, but there were no eyes, no noses, in fact no features of any kind. Although they were obviously sightless, something about the light the ball shed affected them and they backed away from it. The light began to die when the ball fell to the ground, and as it did they moved forward again. Eddie realized they were facing the Kingdom's deadliest enemy—the Warriors of the Black Shroud.

Through both instinct and training the knights had moved close to one another. The king lined them up on either side of him, using only hand signals to convey his orders. Then, with their lances pointing in front of them, they charged the Shroud's front line. Slowly at first and then faster and faster the unicorns pounded toward the enemy. What with the sound of their hooves, the howling of the wind, and the crashes of thunder, the noise was overwhelming. Eddie hung on for dear life. The animals were so close together that he could feel the bodies of unicorns on either side, could smell their sweat and see their eyes wide with fear. If the noise was deafening, the light was blinding. With the lances so near one another they seemed to shine with an even greater intensity.

Onward the unicorns galloped toward the enemy's line, and just as they got to within striking distance the Warriors of the Black Shroud parted and let them gallop through into the darkness beyond. By the light of the lances Eddie could see the faint outline of two Warriors, one to the left and one to the right. Each had an arm raised like a baseball pitcher about to throw. There was an earsplitting hissing noise as their fingertips shot shafts of extreme blackness that could be clearly seen even in the darkness of Diabolonia.

"Darkning bolts!" the king yelled out in warning, but there was nothing that could be done. The bolts were the opposite of explosions, sucking in whatever they hit and making it disappear into the blackness.

Knights from both ends of the line turned their steeds and raced toward the enemy, but their lances proved useless. The Warriors hurled bolt after bolt and destroyed the shining spears one by one, except for the lance Leukos held. The Nebulites' weapon that had proved so deadly in the Battle of Barren Plains could not overcome the power of darkness now. When the last lance was gone the monsters aimed at the knights themselves, and as the bolts found their targets both unicorns and riders simply disappeared. Soon only the king and the knight to his right remained. There was another hissing sound and the knight turned his head toward his monarch. Eddie could see both fear and resignation in his face.

"Farewell, my—" was all he could say before he vanished too.

"No!" cried the king. "No, no, Valoris, my old friend. Not you!"

Suddenly the winds dropped and the thunder ceased. All was total silence. It scared Eddie more than the uproar of noise that had preceded it. Then in the light shed by the king's lance Eddie could just make out another figure. He was the same size as a Nebulite, but was dressed from head to toe in a long black robe. His hood had an opening cut out for the mouth, but none for the eyes. Over it he wore a crown made of black metal inset with jet-black stones. It was the Black Count.

Upon seeing his old master, Tonar reared up in fear, almost unseating the king, and sending Eddie tumbling to the ground. He lay there for a moment trying to regain the breath that had been knocked out of him. An echoing voice rang out across the silence.

"Yes, you fool, he and all your other intruders will be my slaves. How dare you come into my territory? Diabolonia is mine and mine alone. I have left you alone in your pitiful circle of light, but now I will unleash such terrors upon your Kingdom that the light shall never shine again and eternal darkness will be mine to rule forever. Your knights are now my slaves, but you I will not enslave; you I must destroy. Your body will lie undiscovered in the wastes of this barren land, and I will tell your subjects that you deserted them in their hour of greatest need. Warriors, destroy this fool."

Another barrage of darkning bolts rained down. Eddie watched, horrified, as each one came closer to the king. It was as if they were playing with him, torturing him in the last moments of his life. The king must have felt it too because, with a roar of anger, he lowered his lance into the fighting position and spurred Tonar on toward the Count.

"Kill him now!" the Count cried.

The barrage of darkning bolts resumed. Tonar dived to one side to avoid one that struck the ground on his left, but in so doing he moved into the path of another that hit the king squarely in the chest. The monarch's mirrored shield flew into the air and his lance clattered uselessly to the ground. He slumped forward onto Tonar's neck and the animal skidded to a halt.

Complete silence followed; nothing moved and no winds blew. Then the eerie calm was shattered by one long, shrill laugh from the Count, who turned on his heel and departed. The earth rumbled again as the Warriors followed him, and gradually the sound of their monstrous footsteps receded and all was quiet again. Eddie emerged from behind a rock and approached the unicorn. The animal pawed the ground and blew anxiously through his nostrils.

It was almost totally dark now. The only light came from Eddie himself; the king's body cast none at all. He took the reins and stroked Tonar's neck.

"Be still, good friend," Eddie said. "We can do nothing for him now but take him home."

He was almost too frightened to look at the king, and when he did he saw the same wise old man's face that he had known for so long, except that the eyes, those piercing eyes, were dull and sightless. When the darkning bolt hit and Leukos didn't disappear into slavery along with his knights, Eddie feared the king was dead. Now he knew it beyond all doubt. For a moment it seemed as if the life had gone out of Eddie as well.

"Your Majesty," he said, "how will I ever repay all the kindness you have shown me for such a long time? I loved you more than anyone I ever knew."

He felt the tears rising up in his eyes and he brushed them away, for a true soldier never cried on the field of battle. He took the reins and began to walk disconsolately away when he heard a voice in the air all around him. It was the king's voice, but it didn't come from his body.

"Help the Chosen One save the Kingdom," it said.

"The secret of the Source will be his, and yours too, my faithful prince."

And the silence returned.

Eddie set off once more, but he had gone only a few yards when Tonar started to pull him in another direction. In his dazed state he realized that he had no idea how to get back to the Kingdom. In the darkness there was nothing to show him the way, but he knew he could trust the unicorn to take them back.

Slowly and sadly they continued their journey. There were times when he panicked and feared that Tonar had no more idea of the way than he did. Also his feet hurt from walking on the rough terrain. He wore the only shoes he owned, a pair of sneakers that he'd found discarded in an Outerworld landfill. The soles had been thin when he first got them, and now the sharp rocks easily cut through them.

He was at his most despairing when at last he saw the road, and the faint glow on the horizon that could only come from one place. The unicorn hadn't let him down, and soon they would be behind the safety of the walls. He looked back at the king's body. It still lay slumped over Tonar's neck, the feet held firmly in the stirrups. He couldn't imagine what the Kingdom would be like without him, but the thought of it filled him with dread.

CHAPTER 13

Walker and Frankie left the unicorn farm and rode Lightning to the center of the Kingdom. They were eager to find Eddie and show her to him. When they got back to the Palace there was still no sign of him. Astrodor was in the courtyard playing cards with one of the other pages. He had little to do while the king was away.

"Don't worry," he reassured them. "You never know where Prince Edward is. He pretty much comes and goes as he pleases. He may be back already. Why don't you ask

Fussingham? He usually knows everyone's whereabouts. Nice animal, by the way," he added, looking admiringly at Lightning. "She's one of the king's special herd."

"Let's go and see if we can find Fussingham," Walker said to Frankie.

"If you were a real lord you'd help a poor maiden like me get off this beast," she replied.

"I can't dismount until you dismount," Walker pointed out.

As he said the word "dismount," Lightning went down on her front legs so that Walker could step off her quite easily.

"You can now," Frankie chuckled. "Well done, girl."

Walker offered Frankie his hand with an exaggerated bow, but she leaped off by herself in a most unladylike manner.

"Can I leave Lightning here?" Walker asked Astrodor.

"Who? Oh, the unicorn, sure," said Astrodor. "Nobody'll touch a Silverstreak. They're only for royalty."

When he heard this Walker was both pleased and uncomfortable. He loved the Kingdom, and if he was being really honest he would have to admit that he loved being thought of as special, but he still couldn't see himself staying here and becoming the next king. Even though he realized his parents didn't miss him when he was in the Kingdom, he missed them. He would love to be able to tell his mother about Lightning, and Astrodor and the King and Jevon and all the other people he had met, but he knew if he did she would just think it was his overactive imagination at work.

Grabbing Frankie's hand he ran toward the Royal Apartments, pulling her after him. They then raced each other up the stairs, and as they entered the antechamber they collided with Fussingham, knocking the book he always carried out of his hands and sending his quill pen flying.

"Oh my goodness!" he cried as he gathered up his treasured possessions. "Bless me. You young people—you have so much energy. It always happens when we have visitors from the Outerworld. They just get so charged up. I remember one young boy, it must have been two Eons ago—or was it three? No, I think it was two—"

"Fussingham," Walker interrupted, "have you seen Prince Edward?"

"Why, no, not for some time," Fussingham answered. "Let me look in the 'Comings and Goings' entries for the last few cycles."

He opened the book and ran his fingers through the pages.

"Well, as far as I can make out, he didn't leave for the Outerworld," he assured them. "Whenever anyone makes that journey it's automatically recorded in the Book of the Kingdom."

"If he's still here, where would he be?" asked Walker. "Where does he usually go?"

"I'm afraid there's nothing usual about Prince Edward," Fussingham grumbled. "One never knows where he might be."

Suddenly Jevon entered the room with a solemn look on his face.

"Lord Walker, you're back, and just in time!" he said. "Come with me. We must hurry."

"What's happened?" asked Walker.

"We will know more when we get to the gates. Come quickly," Jevon urged.

All three ran down the stairs and out into the court-yard. Jevon's own unicorn was there and he yelled "Mount up!" as he raced toward it. The creature fell to its knees and he vaulted on. Walker tried to do the same with Lightning, but he and Frankie got in each other's way as they both tried to get on at once, and by the time they were mounted Jevon was already galloping down the avenue toward the gates. As they chased behind him

Walker quickly realized why unicorns from the king's herd were called Silverstreaks. Within seconds they had caught up with Jevon and in no time were ahead of him.

A group of Lightkeepers had already gathered in front of the gates by the time they got there. Lumina sat erect on her unicorn with a stern look on her face. Jevon rode straight up to her, and Walker, who was not quite sure what was expected of him, turned to follow.

"What news, my lady?" Jevon asked.

"Not good, I fear, Lord Jevon," she replied. "The sentry saw only two returning, one on foot, and the other slumped over his mount. They should be here shortly."

There was a sudden grinding noise and slowly the massive gates groaned open. Out of the darkness came Eddie, his head bowed, leading Tonar by the reins, with the king's body collapsed over the animal's neck. As they got closer to the gates Eddie stood more erect. All eyes were upon him as he solemnly approached Lumina.

"The king is dead, my lady Lumina," he said, his voice quavering.

Despite his determined efforts not to cry, tears were now streaming down his face.

"He is indeed, Prince Edward," Lumina said kindly. "It seems there is nothing we can do for him now, but what of you? Are you injured?"

"I couldn't help him," he continued, ignoring her question. "I wanted to but there was nothing I could do. The Black Shroud was too strong. The Lances of Light were useless against the darkning bolts."

A gasp of amazement went through the crowd at this statement.

"The knights were old. In the hands of younger men they may have been more effective," Lumina suggested.

"No, my lady, I don't think anyone could have fought better against the enemy," Eddie assured her. "It was so hard to watch. . . . I mean they disappeared one by one, and then the Black Count said he would kill the king and let his body rot in Diabolonia, but I couldn't let him stay there. I had to bring him home. I loved him, my lady. He was so good to me and so wise. After my own father died and my mother left, King Leukos was the one I went to. What will happen to the Kingdom now?"

And then he broke down sobbing. Walker and Frankie both jumped from Lightning's back and ran to their friend. Frankie got to him first and put her arms around him.

"It's okay," she said. "We're here."

"The Kingdom will survive, Prince Edward," said Lumina. "As long as we do nothing foolish, it will survive."

Eddie ignored her and turned to Walker.

"I was so scared," he admitted. "I was so scared I couldn't move. I don't know why I'm such a coward, and I really, really try not to be, but it doesn't make any difference."

"It was brave of you to follow the knights into Diabolonia," Walker told him. "I wouldn't have had the courage to do that, and if you hadn't the king's body would still be out there."

"I wasn't brave," Eddie replied. "I was mad at you and Frankie for going off without me and I wanted to do something that would show you . . . well, I'm not sure what it was I wanted to show you, but something."

"It's over now, and you're back safely." Jevon had ridden up beside Eddie. "Give me the king's reins and I will take him back to the Palace. You go with your friends."

"No, my lord," said Walker. "We will all go together."

He took Lightning's reins and brought her up on one side of Tonar. Jevon then dismounted himself and brought his unicorn to the other. When the knights saw this they also got down and joined them, leading their animals. Only Lumina remained mounted and she rode to the front of the group. Slowly and with great dignity, the makeshift procession moved up the avenue toward the Palace, passing silent, somber crowds on either side. They were halfway between the gates and the Palace when they began to hear comments coming from the back section of the spectators.

"Silly old fool. He should never have gone into Diabolonia."

"What'll happen now? The Kingdom's doomed."

"You can't fight the Shroud; they're too powerful."

Once again it was impossible to see exactly where the remarks were coming from, and most of the onlookers appeared to be as shocked and confused by them as the knights were. As the procession approached the Palace the voices stopped, and a heavy silence hung in the air. They entered the courtyard and Lumina turned her unicorn to halt the column.

"Take His Majesty to the Hall of the People," she instructed the knights. "Lay his body out in a manner that is fitting for a great ruler, and prepare him so that his subjects may pay their last respects and homage to their king. When that is done, return to the antechamber.

We must gather an emergency meeting of the Council of Lightkeepers."

She dismounted, handing her unicorn to a waiting page, and strode purposefully up the stairs to the Royal Chambers. The knights headed toward the Hall on the other side of the courtyard, leaving the three friends by themselves. Walker looked at Eddie. He stood with his head bowed, determined not to look at anyone.

"Eddie," Walker said hesitantly, not knowing quite what to say.

"Leave me alone," Eddie muttered under his breath. "Just leave me alone, please."

"But Eddie," Walker persisted, "we're your friends."

"Nobody needs a coward for a friend," he said.

Frankie stepped forward and once again put her arm around him. This time he tried halfheartedly to shake it off, but she was determined.

"Walker's right," she said. "We are your friends, and you're not a coward. You said yourself that there was nothing even the king and the knights that were with him could do, that the Black Count was too powerful, so what could you have done?"

"I could've tried," Eddie answered, "and I should have

tried, but I was scared and I couldn't move. That's the point, not whether I could've done anything. If I were armed with a thousand Lances of Light it would've made no difference. I couldn't move. I let fear control me and I swore I would never let that happen again."

CHAPTER 14

Walker could feel the tension in the air as Lumina called the emergency meeting of the Council of Lightkeepers to order. Eddie was at the meeting because he was the only witness to the king's death, and Frankie was also in the antechamber for no other reason than her determination not to be left out.

"Lightkeepers." Lumina's voice rang out. "Give me your attention."

The room went silent and all eyes were upon her.

Fussingham sat waiting to scribble down every word she uttered, but Luzaro was nowhere to be found.

"We mourn the loss of our beloved sovereign," she went on. "But as we cope with our present grief we have to look to the challenges that lie ahead. We must decide on two things immediately: how we face any further threats from the Black Count, and who will rule the Kingdom as we go forward."

She paused for a moment, scanning the faces of her audience. All eyes were upon her.

"We should think carefully about the future of this realm," she continued. "Maybe we should consider another form of government. Having a king has served us well as long as one as wise and courageous as Leukos held the throne, but since he left no heir perhaps we should ponder other ways of leading our people."

A murmur of surprise and disbelief rippled through the audience, and Walker saw Jevon go rigid with anger. Lumina continued to speak.

"Ever since our victory at the Battle of Barren Plains there has been peace because we allowed the Black Count to roam freely through Diabolonia. That is his realm as Nebula is ours. I would propose that we do nothing to further aggravate the situation. If the Black

Count sees no more incursions into his territory I believe he will leave us alone and we will continue to live as we have, in harmony."

This time a buzz of agreement ran through the crowd.

"Furthermore, I suggest that we elect a committee of leaders from the ranks of the Lightkeepers," she went on, "to deal with the future government of the realm."

"An excellent idea, my lady," said one of the knights, a pompous fellow that Walker had noticed before, "but only if you will agree to lead it."

"I would be happy to, Lord Lucata," Lumina replied, "but only if you also agree to serve upon it with me."

"It would be an honor and a pleasure," he responded.

Jevon could stand this no more. He stood up and faced Lumina.

"My lady, are you not forgetting something?" he asked. "This is a Kingdom, and for good reason. We depend upon the Source for everything we hold dear, but the workings of the Source are mysterious, and only a Chosen One can know its secrets. A committee cannot stand before the Source and benefit from its wisdom. That is why King Leukos sent our messenger far and wide for many Eons searching for a Chosen One like himself, and finally we are blessed to have one among us."

"But this so-called Chosen One, this bearer of the mark," protested Lumina, "is just a child, and a child of the Outerworld at that. What does he know of the Kingdom and its ways?"

She turned to address Walker.

"Tell me, boy," she demanded, "do you know the secrets of the Source?"

"No, ma'am," Walker replied. "His Majesty took me to the Sanctuary and revealed them to me, but said that until I agreed to be king I would not remember them."

"And my understanding is," said Lumina, "that you have no desire to be king. Is this not so?"

Walker looked around him at the many faces of the Lightkeepers, as well as those of his friends and Jevon. He thought of his parents and the world that waited for him at home, but he also thought about the king and Astrodor, Eddie, and Lightning. Suddenly everything became clear to him. He could not fail them. He could not fail his friends. What did he have to lose, anyway? How often would a kid from rural New England get to be the king of anything?

"No, Lady Lumina," he said. "That isn't so. I do want to be king."

As he said this he suddenly felt like he was back with

the king walking down the passages that led to the Sanctuary. It was like watching a movie on fast-forward, but it was also crystal clear, and he remembered everything the king had told him in detail. Then it was over and he was still in the room full of Lightkeepers. His body hadn't moved; only his mind had gone back to the Source with the dead leader.

"You may wish to be king," Lumina said, "but we must decide if you're fit to be king. You bear the mark, but without the secret of the Source what good is that for the Kingdom?"

"I know the secrets," he assured her. "All of them."

"But you just said moments ago that you didn't," she protested. "Which is it to be—do you or don't you?"

Jevon answered for him.

"Lady Lumina," he said, "King Leukos promised the Chosen One that he would remember all that he was told in the Sanctuary only when he decided to become his heir, and that is what has just happened. I submit that as the Guardian of the Secrets and Bearer of the Mark this young man is the only one qualified to lead us. The danger is great, and the peril within the walls may be as grave as it is outside them."

"I am yet to be convinced of the boy's abilities,"

Lumina answered sharply, "and I refuse to believe we're threatened by our own people."

"Not our own people," Jevon corrected her, "but the Nightangels. King Leukos feared that these agents of the Black Count had infiltrated Nebula and would pit neighbor against neighbor. He said they can take any form, and if they were among us now we might not even know. As you know, my lady, strange things have been happening on the streets. You must have seen and heard—"

"Oh, not the Nightangels again!" Lumina said, rolling her eyes. "His Majesty, great leader though he was, had groundless theories about many things," she said. "I would need more evidence of this than I have seen so far."

"My lady," replied Jevon, "I hope you never will see the evidence you require, because if you do it may be too late."

His hope was to remain unfulfilled, for no sooner had he said this than the evidence appeared. Shouts and cries could be heard from the streets outside the Palace. A Lightkeeper standing near one of the windows turned to Lumina with horror on his face.

"My lady, something terrible is happening."

But before she could move toward him to see for

herself, there was a shout behind her and suddenly Walker felt an arm around his neck. A hand that was as thin as a skeleton's pressed the point of a dagger against his throat. Then he heard a voice yell "Grab the girl!" He couldn't move his head because of the knife, but out of the corner of one eye he saw a figure grasp Frankie's arm and lift her clean off her feet.

The figure was dressed in the same white clothing worn by all of Nebula's citizens, but his appeared to be several sizes too large for him. He had almost no flesh on his body, mostly just skin stretched tightly over bones; his head was like a skull with hair and bulging eyes that were a brilliant red. He looked monstrous and yet somehow familiar.

"I have her!" the creature said. "She won't get away!"

Suddenly Astrodor ran toward the monster.

"Father, is that you? What has happened to you? Why are you doing this? Please let her go," he pleaded.

"I'm not your father, you stupid boy," the creature replied. "Your father died two Eons ago. I merely took his form."

Astrodor froze where he stood. His eyes were wide with disbelief. Jevon stepped in front of the person holding Walker, and spoke to him in a calm voice.

"Luzaro, release the boy and let's talk about this."

"You know me as Luzaro but my name is Thoren, Captain of the Nightangels," replied Walker's captor. "Luzaro, too, met with—shall we say, an unfortunate accident. I took his form hoping to find out the location of the Source but alas, to no avail. Luckily this Chosen One came along just in time, and now he can unlock its secrets."

At that moment a group of Nightangels armed with swords and daggers crashed into the antechamber. They easily pushed their way through the unarmed Light-keepers.

"Take the other child and disarm him," Thoren ordered, "and bring the page as well."

Eddie raised his sword.

"No, I'll die first!" he shouted, swinging the sword over his head in wild circles.

The Nightangels backed away, watching every move that Eddie made. He edged toward Walker, his weapon flailing over his head.

"Move in and get him," Thoren ordered.

With their swords held out in front of them four of the Nightangels began to close in on the boy. One of them thrust a sword into the path of Eddie's blade, and there was a clanging sound and a shower of sparks as metal met metal. Eddie managed to hold on to his weapon, but the clash allowed the other three Nightangels to close in. One of them grabbed his wrist and disarmed him, while another put an arm around his neck and pulled him to the ground. He continued to struggle, kicking out at his enemies with all his might, but it was useless, and he was taken captive.

The Nightangels dragged all three of their prisoners into the king's bedroom. When guards were in place at the doorway Thoren released Walker, while still pointing the dagger at his neck.

"Well, Chosen One," he growled, "your memory returned just in time. Lead us to the Source now that you remember how to get there."

"Don't do it!" yelled Eddie.

"Silence!" roared Thoren.

The Nightangel holding him slapped a skeletal hand across Eddie's mouth, and the boy gagged. The stench of decay that came from every one of their captors hung heavily in the bedroom.

"What if I don't take you," Walker said, trying to sound brave and defiant. "What if I tell you to go jump off a cliff."

"Then you would cause the long, slow, and painful deaths of your friends, one by one, and in front of your eyes," Thoren assured him. "We have ways of killing that make eternal slavery seem like a pleasant vacation. We would start with the girl first, and since you're such a sensitive soul, I wager you'll give in before we're even halfway through."

Walker looked at Frankie. She had already tried to bite Astrodor's "father" and had given a hefty kick to his shins, but nothing had any effect. Walker realized that if it weren't for him she wouldn't be in this mess in the first place.

"So for their sakes," Thoren continued, "it would be best if you could remember everything that old fool Leukos told you."

Walker paused for a minute before answering.

"If I take you there," he asked Thoren, "what's in it for me? What do I get?"

"You get to see your friends live," Thoren replied.

"I don't care about them," Walker said. "They're not really my friends. I don't have friends; I've never had friends. No, I've been thinking. If I can't be king I want to be a Nightangel. I've always been a loser, and for once in my life I want to be on the winning team, on the team that has the power. That's the deal. I'll take you to the Source, but you have to do that for me."

The other children looked at him in stunned silence. Then Eddie pulled the hand away from his mouth and yelled at Walker.

"You traitor; you coward. I wish I'd never seen you and that stupid mark. I wish you'd died—no—I wish you'd never been born. If I ever . . ."

The Nightangel clamped his hand back on Eddie's mouth and roughly shoved him to his knees. Frankie stared at Walker.

"Please don't do it, Walker," she begged. "Please!"

"Well, well," chuckled Thoren. "You may be a smarter young man than I imagined. Of course the Black Count is the only one who can make such a decision, but if you help us I think he would be agreeable."

"Okay," said Walker. "I'll take you to the Source. No need to bring these three along. They'll only get in the way and try to cause trouble."

"Agreed," said Thoren.

He ordered two of the Nightangels guarding the door to join him, and the three of them waited for Walker to lead them to the most secret Sanctuary of the Source.

CHAPTER 15

Well, boy," growled Thoren. "Let's get started. I know we go from here. The king's servant sees many things."

"The unicorn's ear," said Walker. "You have to grasp the unicorn's ear."

He pointed toward the heraldic carving on the far wall. It was in the form of a shield with the sun-shaped symbol of the Kingdom in the lower half, above which were two crossed swords. The top part depicted a unicorn's head with a crown around its neck. The animal's left ear was the only part of the carving that stood out enough to get a hand around. Thoren raced toward the shield, grabbed hold of the ear, and pulled with all his might. Nothing happened.

"I warn you," he snarled, "don't play games with me."

Walker said nothing but walked toward the carving himself. When he took hold of the ear, which he could barely reach, the wall silently revolved to reveal another room, smaller than the bedroom.

"The way to the Source is open only to a Chosen One," Walker explained.

"I'm so glad we have one, then," sneered Thoren, grabbing hold of Walker's arm and dragging him into the room, followed closely by the other two Nightangels. Once everybody was inside, the wall slid back into its closed position. Thoren whirled around, his dagger at the ready.

"This had better not be a trap!" he cried. "If it is it will be the last one you set."

"Why would I want to trap you, sir?" Walker said respectfully. "Remember, I'm on your side. I told you, I want to join the Nightangels."

"But there is no way out of this," Thoren observed, looking around the room. "Where do we go from here?"

Walker went to the far left-hand corner of the room and turned back toward Thoren.

"We go this way," he said, as he walked through the wall and disappeared. The three Nightangels ran toward what appeared to be a solid wall, but it was merely a trick of light, a projection of the room's glow that hid a narrow opening.

They found Walker waiting for them in a passageway that spiraled down in broad sweeps, going deep belowground. Thoren strode ahead of them, and as the other Nightangels prodded Walker forward they noticed a strange thing happening. The farther the boy went the brighter he glowed.

"That's good," Thoren remarked when they pointed this out. "That must mean we're on the right path."

They had gone no more than a few feet when he seemed to be proven wrong. The passageway suddenly stopped in a dead end. Thoren went up to its face and inspected it carefully. It looked like solid rock. There were no seams, cracks, or any other indication that it had ever moved or ever would.

"I assume," he said to Walker, "there is a solution to this."

"Yes, sir," Walker replied. "A very simple one."

He walked up to the rock face and placed his hand upon it. A rumbling noise started and vibrations began to shake the passageway. Then, slowly, the end of the tunnel began to open. As it did a bright light flooded the passageway, temporarily blinding them with its intensity. When their eyes adjusted they saw that the light came from the walls, floor, and ceiling of a large room, empty except for another carving of the same heraldic shield that they had first seen in the Royal Chambers.

"We are at the Sanctuary," Walker said, "but for the next part I need the help of you two gentlemen."

He turned to his escort of Nightangels.

"Do whatever he says," Thoren ordered impatiently.

"You must lift me up," Walker instructed the two creatures, "and place the mark on my cheek next to the eye of the unicorn."

The Nightangels were strong and with one on either side of him they easily lifted Walker up and did as he said. As his birthmark came close to the carved eye a piercing alarm began to sound, and slowly one entire wall of the room began to rise. The alarm became louder, and light of an unimaginable brilliance shone through the opening.

When the wall was completely open the alarm stopped,

but its shrill sound was replaced by the scream of the Nightangels. They pressed their hands over their eyes and stumbled blindly around in front of the Source, bumping into one another. They grabbed on to one another's clothing or put their arms out to steady themselves, and Walker saw that their eyes had lost all their brilliant red color and now were horrific milky spheres protruding from their sockets.

"You ordered me to remember all the secrets the king told me and I did," he said. "One of them was that only a Chosen One could withstand the light of the Source. All others will be blinded by its brilliance. That's why it was important that Frankie and Eddie didn't come with us."

Thoren turned his head toward Walker's voice. The pain seemed to have passed and he stood still and calm.

"What a clever boy you are!" he sneered. "But maybe not as clever as you think. Remember, all our masters, the Count and the Warriors, are sightless, as we are now. And when the light is finally extinguished from this realm then it will be we who have the advantage, for eyes will not help you in the blackness of Diabolonia."

"This realm will never lose its light," Walker said defiantly. "The Source will live forever."

"Nothing lives forever, boy," Thoren said. "Remember

that, and remember there is more than one way of seeing."

Walker suddenly realized the other two Nightangels had stopped stumbling around in panic and had regained Thoren's same deadly calm. Now all three of them were moving toward him. He moved to the right but so did they, all the time getting closer. There was a small space between two of the Nightangels, and Walker made a run for it. Sensing his movement the Nightangel reacted fast, but Walker had the energy of the Source pulsing through him and he felt the brush of the beast's fingers as it snatched at him and missed.

Walker backed into the passageway that led from the Sanctuary back to the king's bedroom.

"You think you can catch me?" he yelled. "You'll never catch a Chosen One. It'd take more than stinky old bags of bones like you to capture the Bearer of the Mark."

With a roar Thoren lurched toward him, followed by the other two. As they did, the walls of the Sanctuary closed behind them. Walker knew he had to time it carefully. The walls closed when he went through them, and if he got it right he could trap his pursuers behind the last one into the king's bedroom.

He had a good lead, enough for him to open the

bedroom wall and give it time to close before Thoren and the others could get through it. But then another idea struck him. What was he thinking? How stupid could he be? Even if he got through the wall and it closed, trapping the Nightangels in the passageway, he would end up in a Palace full of their cohorts who could still see and who were armed.

There was nothing to do but to press on and find out what would happen. His heart pounding, he pushed gently on the place he knew would open the heavy wall. It slowly swung away to reveal a scene of utter chaos.

The room was thick with people. Almost all the Lightkeepers present in the antechamber were now packed inside the bedroom. Everyone was agitated and shouting, but as the wall swung open silence gradually descended. Jevon pushed his way to the front of the crowd, followed by Frankie, who could push as well as anyone.

"Walker, what happened?" the knight asked. "Are you all right?"

"I'm fine," Walker assured him. He told Jevon all that had happened in the Sanctuary, and how he had remembered the king's warning that only a Chosen One's eyes could withstand the light of the Source.

Frankie ran up and threw her arms around him in an enormous hug.

"Oh, Walker," she cried, "I'm so glad you didn't join the enemy. I never thought you would, of course, but you were so brave to go with those awful people by yourself just so you could save us."

Because Walker hadn't yet entered the bedroom the wall was still open, and Thoren came stumbling out, yelling at the top of his voice.

"Nightangels, your assistance. We need your assistance."

"That will do you no good, Luzaro, or whatever you call yourself," said Jevon. "Your friends are as sightless as you. At the moment you lost your vision they also lost theirs. They are our prisoners now."

"No," groaned Thoren. "That cannot be."

"Why would they all go blind at the same moment?" asked Walker.

"Who knows with these creatures?" said Jevon. "They are not like us. Maybe what happens to one happens to them all. Come, let's gather them into one group where we can keep an eye on them all."

He took Thoren's hand and roughly pulled him forward. The crowd parted as he moved the three prisoners through it with Frankie and Walker following them. When they got to the antechamber they saw that Lumina was seated on the throne that the king usually occupied. In front of her, knights with their swords drawn guarded a large group of Nightangels. The three that had accompanied Walker to the Source were added to its number.

"My lord Jevon," Lumina said, "are we any closer to solving the mystery of what happened here?"

Jevon told her all he knew about what happened, and as he did Eddie and Astrodor sidled up to Walker and Frankie.

"See," Frankie whispered loudly to Eddie, "I told you he wasn't a traitor. I knew he had a plan."

"I'm sorry I doubted you, Walker," Eddie whispered back. "But you were pretty convincing."

"I had to be," said Walker quietly.

He would have added more but he realized that an argument had broken out between Lumina and Jevon.

"But my lady," Jevon said forcefully, "he has proven that he has courage and is resourceful and has also shown the value of the secrets of the Source that he alone knows. Why do you insist he should not be king? He has every qualification."

"We are grateful for his bravery," Lumina replied. "But

these are dangerous times, Lord Jevon, and the Council and I agree that we should not place our future in the hands of an untried child from the Outerworld."

"May I remind my lady that he is a Chosen One and we have always been led by a Chosen One?" Jevon growled.

"And I would remind you, Lord Jevon, that I am the Leader of the Lightkeepers and head of our new Ruling Council," she answered back, "and we have decided that this boy will not be our king."

CHAPTER 16

Because there was no daylight in the Kingdom, time there was measured differently from the Outerworld. The nearest equivalent to a day the citizens called a cycle, although exactly how they calculated one Walker was never quite sure. But in the cycles that followed the defeat of the Nightangels many changes took place.

The first was the expulsion of the enemies in their midst. The defeated Nightangels, about sixty in total, were gathered by the Kingdom's main gates along with a large crowd of spectators. They no longer radiated light, and stumbled forward in a line, each with an arm on the shoulder of the one in front. The massive stone doors finally swung apart and a blast of icy cold air swept in through the gap. At that moment Thoren, who was at the head of the line, suddenly stood erect and turned his head toward where he sensed the crowd was assembled.

"You fools!" he cried. "Do you think that this little victory you have claimed over us will mean you are safe forever? When the dark descends upon this realm we will return."

Then he led the Nightangels into the wilderness that waited for them outside the walls. Walker and his friends stood and watched until the gates closed again. They didn't know what would happen next, or indeed what to do next, so they wandered back to the Palace. Walker led Lightning by the reins, but even she seemed dispirited. When they got to the courtyard no plan of action sprang into their minds and they sat on the edge of the fountain aimlessly swinging their legs.

The citizens they saw were in a strange mood. Given how close the Kingdom had come to disaster they appeared remarkably cheerful. Jugglers juggled, musicians played, and everyone looked as if they were having a fine time but somehow their good spirits didn't ring true to Walker. Normally people passed by the street entertainers, maybe pausing for a while before moving on. It was rare to see a crowd of more than eight or ten watching. Now there were dozens, and every time a juggler did even the simplest trick there were roars of applause. The laughter was too loud, and the smiles too broad. Frankie felt it too.

"Everyone's acting very weird," she observed. "It's like everything is normal, but it can't be, can it?"

"I doubt it," said Eddie. "Thoren was pretty mad, and I bet he'll make good on his threats, or rather the Black Count will. They'll be back, you see if I'm not right."

"Nobody here seems worried about that," remarked Frankie.

"These people have only ever known peace," Eddie told her. "They have no idea how to deal with anything else."

"That's all *I've* ever known too," Frankie protested, "but when Thoren said what he said, well, it got my attention, I can tell you."

Frankie suddenly turned to Walker.

"Since it doesn't seem like you're going to be king anytime soon," she said, "how do you feel about a trip back to the old country?"

"Which old country?" Walker asked, confused.

"Our old country—the Outerworld," she replied. "You know—the good old US of A. I've got things to do, and my clothes are starting to smell really yucky."

It was true that they still wore the same garments they had arrived in, but it wasn't the thought of new clothes that made the idea of going back to the Outer-world appealing to Walker. It seemed that after all the fuss they'd made nobody wanted him to be king after all. Well, he would leave them to it. If they could get on without him—fine. If not, let them beg him to come back.

"Okay," he said. "I'm up for it. You coming, Eddie?"

"No way!" exclaimed Eddie. "You can't leave now. Anything could happen and I need to be here. We might need you too."

"In that case you know where to find me," Walker assured him. Then he stopped for a minute. *Lightning! What would happen to Lightning?*

"Um, Eddie," he said in a more subdued tone. "Would you look after my unicorn while I'm away? I don't think she'll be much trouble."

"I suppose so," Eddie grumbled. "At least you'll come back for her if you wouldn't come back for anyone else. Go on, get out of here."

"Thanks, Eddie," Walker said. "Come on, Frankie, let's go."

Walker was getting much better at landing and they materialized a few feet from the far side of the barn. Although the landing was good, the weather was bad; they had arrived in the middle of a heavy downpour. Frankie held her arms out like the wings of a plane and ran in circles, yelling at the top of her lungs.

"It feels so good!" she cried.

"It's great to be back, isn't it?" he asked Frankie. "Even in the rain."

"Especially in the rain," she said. "I never thought much about rain until I went somewhere there isn't any."

They stood at the barn door taking in deep breaths of warm, moist air that smelled of vegetation and earth—that smelled like home, in fact.

"I've got to go back to my house and get out of these things," Frankie finally said. "Do you want to come by later?"

"Sure," Walker agreed.

They parted and made their soggy ways home.

* * *

Walker entered the house through the kitchen door. His mother was sitting at the table reading the newspaper and having a cup of coffee.

"Walker!" she exclaimed. "You're soaked! Go upstairs right now and get out of those wet clothes."

When he returned to the kitchen a few minutes later his mother looked at him and chuckled.

"You know, my son," she said, "I don't think you'll ever have a career in the fashion industry."

He had put on two T-shirts, one of which was back-to-front, and neither of which was fully tucked into his pants. The pants themselves his mother had put aside to take to the local thrift shop because they were too small for him and came halfway up his shins. He'd taken the first two socks that came to hand out of the drawer. One was blue and the other gray. He didn't exactly look like a king.

"I thought I'd go over to Frankie's house, if that's okay with you," he said to his mother.

"Okay with me?" his mother cried. "It's more than okay with me. I'm delighted you've found someone you like to play with."

The rain turned out to be just a heavy shower that soon ended and so Walker headed out in the direction of Frankie's house. As he opened the gate and started up the path, the front door flew open and Frankie ran toward him and enveloped him in a huge hug.

"I'm glad you're here," she said. "I missed you."

"We've only been apart for about an hour," he protested.

"You don't have to be apart from someone for a long time to miss them," she assured him. "Anyway, be glad that I miss you."

"I am," he said, and he was.

"Let's go down in the basement," she suggested. "It's all dusty and spooky down there, and you can imagine there are bodies of people who were murdered long ago bricked up in the walls."

This didn't make it sound like the most fun place to spend time, but Walker followed her down anyway. When they got there it turned out to be far less sinister than she had described it. There was a brand-new furnace with shiny copper pipes leading to various parts of the house. Along one wall was her father's wine collection all neatly stacked in wooden racks. The only daylight filtered in through tiny slit windows at the top of the walls, and at the far end steps led up to large red metal doors that opened the cellar up to the outside world. It wasn't spooky as much as boring, and Walker had no idea what they would do to pass the time.

But passing time was never a problem for Frankie. Talking was one of her favorite activities. She described in detail her bedroom in Boston and the advantages it had over the one in the cottage; she told him about the annoying characteristics of her girlfriends and how she thought she probably liked boys better; she talked about her swimming coach, her favorite music, and the book she just read. Then she suddenly asked him:

"If they don't want you to be king, will you go back to Nebula?"

The question surprised Walker because he had never considered not returning, no matter how disheartened he was by what had happened.

"Yes, of course," he replied.

"I think we should," Frankie agreed. "They need you, even if they don't know it. If it wasn't for you the Night-angels would still be there, and who knows what would've happened by now. Anyway, I like Eddie even though he can be a pain, and he doesn't have many friends. I think we may be the only ones he's got."

This surprised Walker. He hadn't thought of Eddie being lonely or friendless. He always seemed so confident, yet when he came to think about it Walker realized that they were probably the closest companions Eddie had.

"So when do you think we should go back?" asked Frankie.

"Let's give it a while," said Walker, who still hoped Lumina would realize what a mistake she had made and would beg him to return.

No sooner had he said this than they heard the sound of knocking on one of the windows. They looked up to see Eddie's worried face peering through the slit.

"Eddie," Frankie shouted, "what are you doing there?"

Eddie said something in reply, but they couldn't hear what it was and he couldn't hear Frankie, however loudly she yelled, and she could yell.

"It's no use," she said. "We're going to have to open the cellar doors and let him in."

Walker opened the doors and Eddie came down the steps, his sword clanking against each one as he descended. Just then they heard Frankie's mother calling down the stairwell that led into the house.

"What's happening down there?" she asked. "Frances, what are you doing in the basement?"

"Nothing, Mom!" Frankie yelled. "Walker thought he heard a ghost and we went to check it out. It's okay, there's nothing here; we're phantom-free."

They heard Frankie's mother sigh as she walked away.

"What's up, Eddie?" Walker asked, worried by the grim look on his friend's face.

"You have to come back," Eddie said. "You can't believe what's been going on since you left."

"But that was like a couple of hours ago," protested Frankie. "What could possibly happen in such a short time?"

"Frankie, you have to remember," Eddie said impatiently. "Time here and there are totally different, and believe me, there's been enough time for plenty to happen in the Kingdom, and none of it's good."

CHAPTER 17

S he's gone nuts," said Eddie.

"Who has?" asked Walker.

"Lumina," replied Eddie. "I think this thing with the Nightangels has made her crazy. She's got the Lightkeepers under her thumb and they do whatever she tells them, and she tells them some pretty stupid things."

"Like what?" Frankie asked.

"Well, they just passed a recommendation that nobody think negative thoughts, and that to do so would mean a period of reorientation in the stone quarry," Eddie said.

Recommendations were the Nebula equivalent of laws, but during the king's rule there had been no punishments other than the disapproval of your fellow citizens, which had generally been enough to make an offender mend his or her ways.

"How can they know what someone's thinking?" asked Frankie.

"They can't," replied Eddie, "but the problem is you can't prove you weren't thinking negatively if someone says you were. She's also put extra locks on the gates, and stopped any more patrols, even the ones that just stand guard on the walls. In fact, nobody's supposed to even look over the walls anymore. She says it's so we don't antagonize the Black Count, and if we keep ourselves to ourselves we can live in harmony with him, which I think is ridiculous."

"This all sounds pretty weird," Walker agreed, "but it doesn't sound serious enough to make you come flying back here."

"That's because you haven't heard the worst of it yet," Eddie assured him. "She locked Jevon in one of the rooms in the palace, because, guess what, he's been thinking negative thoughts. What she really means is he disagrees with her."

"Jevon's under house arrest?" gasped Frankie.

"More like room arrest," Eddie said. "He has a guard outside his door all the time, and nobody's allowed to see him. The Kingdom's never been like this before. Lumina says she's doing everything to make the citizens feel more secure and happy, but it's had the opposite effect. Everyone's nervous and jumpy and suspicious."

"But what can we do?" Walker asked.

"I don't know," Eddie admitted, "but whatever it is, you can't do it from here. You have to come back."

Walker and Frankie looked at each other. Frankie shrugged her shoulders.

"He's right, you know. We have to at least try," Frankie said. "No way we can leave Jevon wasting away in a prison cell."

Walker thought this was a bit overdramatic but he agreed with her. They had to go back and help Jevon and the Kingdom. At least they'd both had a change of clothes.

Upon landing in Nebula the first thing Walker wanted to do was get Lightning. Eddie had left her in the care of the Mistress of the Herd while he went to the Outerworld.

"About time you came back," she snapped at Walker. "She's been nervous and skittish the entire time she's been here. That may be because she's been missing you, or it may be that she's picking up a lot of the nonsense that's happening now. Unicorns are very sensitive, you know."

Lightning did seem pleased to see Walker, which in turn pleased him. He thought three of them were too heavy to ride her, so they walked back to the square in the middle of the Palace with Walker leading Lightning by the reins.

Nebula looked no different from when they had left it, but there was a tension under it all that you didn't need to be a unicorn to feel. The laughter was too loud, the play too frantic, and every so often Walker caught people giving one another nervous glances, as if to make sure they weren't doing anything that would cause their neighbors suspicion.

"Well, now that we're here, what are we going to do?" Frankie asked.

"We have to see Jevon," said Walker.

"Oh yeah, that's a great idea!" snorted Frankie. "Except for the guard in front of his door twenty-four-seven."

"We've got to find a way to do it," Walker insisted.

"Well," said Eddie, "there may be a way. Nebulites have never had to guard people before and I suspect they aren't very good at it. If we can distract him I bet we could slip past him."

"Let me do that," said Frankie. "My mom says I'm very distracting."

They followed Eddie down a flight of stairs to the part of the Palace that was belowground. The steps curved around in a spiral until they opened out into a long passageway with rooms on either side. In each room there was a large table with men and women working on piles of paper. At the end of the passage Eddie stopped.

"Peek around this corner and you'll see the guard," he whispered.

Walker and Frankie peered carefully around the edge of the wall. At the end of the passage was a guard holding a short lance. He looked bored, and was using the point of his weapon to draw patterns in the dust on the floor. He stood in front of a huge stone door.

Frankie looked at the others and indicated to them to follow her. She went into a nearby room that was empty except for papers stacked along the walls.

"Okay," she whispered, "here's the plan. You two stay in here and duck out of sight. I'll get the guard away from his post. That'll give you time to get into Jevon's room. How you get out is your problem."

She picked up some papers from one of the piles, and put a worried look on her face. Then she left the room and headed down the passage in the direction of the guard.

"Stop, you. Miss, what are you doing here?" shouted the guard.

Eddie rolled his eyes and whispered to Walker. "He's supposed to say: 'Halt, who goes there?'"

Then they heard Frankie give a little shriek as if she had been startled.

"Oh, I'm sorry," she said. "I didn't see you there."

"You're the Outerworld girl, aren't you?" questioned the guard.

"Yes," Frankie agreed. "My name is Frances Livonia Hayes, but you can call me Frankie. You can also help me, because I'm lost."

"Where are you trying to get to?" the guard asked.

"I have to go to the Department of Citizen Affairs," she replied.

"What business do you have there?" he inquired.

"Lady Lumina told me to go there. I have to fill out some papers," she answered.

At the sound of Lumina's name the guard's attitude changed completely.

"Oh, yes, of course," he said. "Lady Lumina—of course. Well, it's easy enough. Turn around and walk to the end of this passage and make a right. Go all the way down the next one and when it stops make a left and you'll see the Department immediately on your right."

"I'm sorry," Frankie said, "but I don't understand when you say left and right. Those words mean something completely different in the Outerworld."

"They do?" the guard asked in amazement. "How do you give directions, then?"

"Oh, we just say 'klink' or 'klunk,'" Frankie informed him. "We would say: 'Go to the crossroads and make a klink'—or a klunk, whichever was correct."

The two listening boys had to stifle snorts of laughter.

"Well, let me show you," said the guard. "This is your left hand."

"This one?" asked Frankie.

"No, that's your right," he said. "Turn around and face in the same direction as me. Now that's your left—got it?"

"It's all very confusing," said Frankie with a sigh. "Do you think you could just show me where the office is?"

"I can't leave my post," he told her.

"I'm sure Lady Lumina would be very grateful if you took me there. She said it was most important that I fill out these forms," Frankie said.

There was a pause.

"All right," the guard said, "but quickly, because I shouldn't leave here."

Then the two boys heard Frankie's and the guard's footsteps coming toward them and they pressed themselves up against the piles of paper and held their breaths. Frankie kept up a continuous stream of chatter and then she and her guide passed by the room and continued down the passage.

"Quickly," Eddie muttered. "We don't have much time."

As quietly as possible they raced toward the huge door. They pressed their shoulders against it but it wouldn't budge.

"It's locked!" Eddie exclaimed.

"Maybe not," said Walker, pointing to the dust on the floor. "Look at those marks. It opens out toward us."

Sure enough, there was a large quarter-circle marked in the dust where the door had been dragged open. The only problem was that there was no handle or anything else that you could pull. Walker thought for a minute.

"Sometimes," he said, "less force works better than more."

And with that he gave the door a little push with his hand, and it started to groan open by itself. It revealed a small room with no windows and just a stone table with a bench in front of it. Jevon was sitting on it with his back to the door. When he heard it open he turned toward them.

"How did you two get in here?" he cried. "Where's the guard?"

"He's busy showing Frankie the way to somewhere she doesn't need to go," said Walker.

But Jevon wasn't even listening to the explanation. He had noticed that the door was starting to slowly close.

"Oh no! Quickly, find something to wedge it open!" he shouted.

But it was too late. The huge stone portal had already slammed shut.

"Well, my young friends," said Jevon, "I'm afraid that means there are now three prisoners in this room. There's no way of opening it from this side. Believe me, I've tried."

"Why is this happening, Jevon?" asked Walker. "What's got into Lumina? She was never very friendly, but I always thought she was okay."

"She's a good woman," Jevon said, "but she's scared, and to tell the truth so are most of the citizens of Nebula. They don't know how to deal with anything that disturbs their peaceful lives. Lumina thinks she can keep the Kingdom safe by making sure that nobody goes into Diabolonia, and anyone who disagrees with her is a threat to the security of the realm and a traitor who has to be silenced. That's why I'm shut in this room right now."

"This has never happened before," complained Eddie. "When King Leukos reigned you could say anything about him, and he didn't care—not that many people did, of course, because they all loved him."

"Leukos was a strong leader," Jevon said, "and strong leaders never fear criticism."

"What can we do, Lord Jevon?" Walker asked anxiously.

"In all honesty, I don't know," said Jevon. "I'm not one to despair, but our situation is grim. In the Eons that have passed since his defeat the Black Count has become stronger and the weapons we used against him then no longer have their power. If only we knew what was happening in Litherium or the other Sister Cities we might be able to form a plan, but if the king and his knights armed with Lances of Light can't get through to them, then who can?"

A despondent silence fell. Then after a few minutes a broad grin gradually replaced the worried frown on Walker's face.

"You know, there may be people who can get through to Litherium," he said.

"How so?" asked Jevon. "The last two attempts both ended in disaster."

"But not everyone was killed or captured," Walker pointed out.

"Only two survived," said Jevon. "A young page and his royal highness here."

"And what did they both have in common?" Walker asked.

"They were both young?" Jevon suggested.

"They were," Walker agreed, "but maybe more importantly they were both short."

"Short yourself," protested Eddie. "I'm as tall as you are."

"Yes," Walker said. "You are, but neither of us is as tall as a man, and we're much shorter than a man on a unicorn."

"So you think the Warriors of the Black Shroud

couldn't see them?" Jevon asked incredulously.

"Well," said Eddie, "we know they can't see, but they know how to aim despite that, trust me."

"But did they aim at you?" asked Walker.

"Hmm." Eddie considered the question thoughtfully. "No, I suppose they didn't."

"Right!" cried Walker. "That's because whatever it is that tells them someone's there couldn't detect you."

"It's a possibility," agreed Jevon, "but only that. You can't be certain."

"No," Walker accepted, "but it's worth a risk."

"Are you suggesting that the two of you should go out there into the wilderness by yourselves without any protection and try to get through to Litherium?" Jevon asked, aghast.

"Can you think of a better plan, my lord?" Walker said. "Or even another one?"

"Well, no," Jevon admitted.

Once again there was silence. Then Jevon sighed and said: "Desperate times demand desperate measures."

"I think it's a great plan," said Eddie, "and the more I think of it the more I'm sure Walker's right. During the fight out there when the king was killed, it was almost as if I didn't exist."

"It doesn't matter whether or not it's a great plan," said Walker, "if we can't get out of this room. And even if we get out of the room we still have to get out of the Kingdom, and with Lumina's new rules that may be a bit tricky."

"Leave the first up to me. I've just thought of something that might get you out of here," Jevon replied. "As for getting out of the Kingdom—there is an observation tower in the farthest part of the wall on the other side of the unicorn herd. It hasn't been used for Eons, and it has a secret stone that opens out to give the watchmen a sheltered place to look out. It's not big enough for an adult to get through, but I'm pretty sure you children could slip through it."

"Pretty sure or completely sure?" Walker asked.

"Not completely," said Jevon, "but if it's too small you've lost nothing and you'll have to think of something else."

The two boys looked at each other for just a moment.

"Are you up for this?" Walker asked Eddie.

"Lead on," his friend replied. "I'm right behind you."

CHAPTER 18

Now," said Jevon, "stand on either side of the door and don't let the guard see you."

Walker stood on the right side of the door and Eddie on the left, and both of them flattened themselves against the wall. When they were in position Jevon banged hard on the door. Walker worried that it would be too thick for the sound to carry, but after a few moments the door opened a crack and the guard peeked in.

"What do you want?" he asked gruffly.

"I wish to see Lady Lumina," Jevon answered. "Please take me to her."

"You may want to see her," the guard replied, "but the question is does she want to see you? And I doubt very much that the answer is yes."

"I want to apologize to her, and to admit my wrong-doings," Jevon said in a humble tone. "Would you please convey this message to her?"

"So, you've seen the error of your ways, have you?" asked the guard smugly. "Well, that's all well and good, but it doesn't mean she'll forgive you just like that. Still, I'll see what I can do."

The door closed, and Eddie looked at Jevon with a worried frown.

"Why did you say that?" he asked. "You've done nothing wrong, so why should you apologize?"

"No, you're right," Jevon agreed. "But nothing short of a groveling apology and admission of guilt is going to get me out of this room, and if I don't get out of this room neither do you. And if you don't get out then the Kingdom is doomed. Let's see what happens when the guard comes back."

"Let's pull this bench over here before he does," said Walker.

"What for?" Eddie asked. "Do you think he'll be in a better mood if we offer him a seat?"

"No," Walker replied irritably. "But if he takes Jevon to Lumina we're going to need something to jam open the door to stop it from closing and leaving us trapped again. There's nothing else here solid or big enough."

"Good idea!" cried Jevon. "Let's do it now."

They lifted the heavy stone bench and placed it by the wall on the side that the door opened. Then there was silence. Nobody said anything until a short time later the door began to open again. The boys pressed themselves against the wall once more. This time the door opened fully, but fortunately the guard didn't enter the room.

"Well," he said, "you're in luck. Her ladyship seems to be in a forgiving mood today. She said to bring you to her and if your apology is sincere then she will consider your fate. Come with me."

Jevon walked out of the room and disappeared with the guard. The door began to swing shut again, but Walker and Eddie jammed the heavy bench into the gap. The door closed against it but could move no farther, allowing the two boys to slip into the passageway and hurry out of the Palace.

"We have to find Frankie," Walker said.

"Don't worry, finding her is easy," replied Eddie. "Losing her is the hard part!"

And indeed as they walked out into the square there she was, stroking Lightning's nose.

"Did it work?" she asked eagerly. "Did you get to see him?"

"We did," Walker assured her. "You were brilliant, by the way."

She gave a quick curtsy.

"Thank you, my lord," she said. "But what did Jevon say? What are we going to do?"

They told her all that had happened and explained the plan to go to Litherium and why Walker thought children would get through where adults failed. She frowned.

"It could be," she said, "but on the other hand it could just be coincidence. I wish we knew for sure."

"We're never going to know for sure until we're on the other side of the walls," Walker said.

"You know, we might get Astrodor to join us," Eddie suggested.

"Why?" Walker asked. "I would've thought the fewer people the less chance there was of getting caught."

"That's true," Eddie agreed, "but Astrodor and his

brothers have been pretty much outcasts since it turned out their father was a Nightangel. His mom came from Litherium and he told me he still has relatives there. Maybe they could take the family in until all this blows over. He lost his job as a page, did I tell you that?"

"Oh no!" cried Walker. "No, you didn't. Poor Astrodor. He so wanted to be a Lightkeeper, and now he's not just lost his dad but he also lost the chance of that happening. But you're right, he should join us if he wants to. Do you know where he is?"

"Not exactly," said Eddie. "But he can't be too far away. Let me go and find him and I'll meet you at the tower."

"Okay," said Walker, "but don't be long. We may not have much time."

Eddie strode off in the direction of Astrodor's house. Walker and Frankie mounted up and headed for the tower. It was strange to ride Lightning through the streets now. Nobody waved to them or stared in admiration at the beautiful unicorn. In fact, nobody stared at them at all, or pointed out Walker's mark to their children and told them in hushed tones that he was a Chosen One. It was almost as if the citizens were embarrassed by the presence of the Outerworld children.

They found the tower easily enough in one of the

bleakest and most desolate parts of the Kingdom. The door was slightly ajar, so they pushed and it swung wide open. Peering inside they saw steps spiraling up. They started to climb them and eventually came to a trapdoor that Walker heaved open. With a little effort they pulled themselves through it and found they were on the top of the tower, surrounded by a turreted wall.

As they looked in one direction there was a thrilling panorama of the entire Kingdom, glowing golden in its own light. You could clearly make out the Palace, the mines, the mill, and the garment factory where the robes everyone wore were produced. When they turned around darkness was the only thing they saw, apart from the light that spilled from the Kingdom. It lit a short distance of that barren land, and revealed a rock-strewn surface that reminded Walker of the pictures of the moon landing in his history book.

Frankie shuddered. "I'm not looking forward to this," she said.

"You don't have to come, you know," Walker said. "Eddie, Astrodor, and I can do it by ourselves."

Frankie narrowed her eyes and looked at him with determination.

"Listen, buster, don't even think of going without me,"

she said. "All I'm saying is I'm not looking forward to it."

"No, you're right," admitted Walker. "Me neither."

They started back down, looking for the opening in the wall that Jevon had told them about. Walker suddenly stopped. He noticed that one of the stones was a different shape from the others, tall and narrow while the rest were squat and square. Tentatively he pushed against it with his hand, and it slid open leaving a slender gap in the wall, not big enough for a fully grown man but one that a child might squeeze through.

"This is still way too high," Frankie said, peering down to the ground. The drop was enough to break legs or sprain ankles upon landing.

"Yes," Walker agreed, "but Jevon's smart. He wouldn't suggest something that was no good. Maybe there are other openings that we didn't see."

They hurried down the stairs, and sure enough every thirty steps or so there was another lookout point, each of them facing out into the black wastes. The lowest of them was only about ten feet from the ground below.

"Do you think we can get through here?" asked Frankie.

"It may be a bit of a squeeze," Walker replied, "but I think we can. Lightning can't come with us, though."

"Oh no," gasped Frankie. "I'd forgotten about Lightning. What're you going to do with her?"

"Jevon said this place is right next to the unicorn herd, so why don't we try to slip her back into it and hope that grumpy old Mistress of the Herd isn't around?" Walker suggested.

"Ugh!" snorted Frankie. "That woman gives me the creeps."

Lightning was waiting patiently outside. Walker took off her saddle and put it in the tower. The two children could see the fences that marked the perimeter of the farm a short distance away and they headed toward them. There was a gate that looked as if it hadn't been opened in some time, but with a lot of effort they finally managed to get it wide enough to push Lightning through. She didn't look happy about being left behind, but soon a group of unicorns came up to her and she trotted off into the large paddock with them. Now there was nothing left for Walker and Frankie to do but go back to the tower and wait for Eddie and Astrodor.

They sat in silence on the staircase until they heard the crunch of footsteps on the dusty ground. The door swung open to reveal Eddie by himself.

"Couldn't you find him?" Walker asked.

"Yeah, I found him, all right," replied Eddie, "but he didn't want to come."

"Oh well," said Frankie. "At least we gave him the chance."

"No, it's not as simple as that," Eddie warned them. "He said he felt duty bound to tell Lumina what we're going to do."

"No!" cried Walker. "Why would he do that?"

"He thinks he can get back into her favor," said Eddie, "and she'll make him a page again and he'll still be able to be a Lightkeeper at some point. He wants to be a knight more than anything. It's all he thinks about."

"Couldn't you stop him?" Frankie demanded.

"I was going to lock him in a room," said Eddie, "but none of those stupid houses have doors."

"There's nothing we can do about it now," said Walker. "Let's get going as fast as we can before anything else goes wrong."

CHAPTER 19

The three children went back up the stairs to the first and lowest of the lookout points. Walker pushed it open and spread out before them was the utter blackness of the world beyond the walls. A shudder ran down his spine.

"This is it, then," he said more bravely than he felt. "No turning back."

The thought ran through his head of taking Frankie's hand and then running as fast as he could until they materialized in the orchard or the barn or the fields near the woods, but instead he pushed his body through the gap until he was sitting with his legs dangling on the outside of the wall.

"I only hope we're doing the right thing," said Walker. "This could be a disaster."

"Yes," agreed Eddie. "It could be, and it probably will be if you think like that. Positive wins the day, and always has!"

And with that ringing in his ears Walker pushed off and landed with a jolt on the rough and stony soil of Diabolonia. Frankie jumped next with considerably more grace and athletic skill than Walker had shown. Then Eddie jumped out, sword in hand. This dangerous gesture was supposed to add a dramatic touch to his descent, but all it did was unbalance him and he landed with a bang, rolling over several times. He got up, brushed himself off, and mustered as much dignity as he could. Then he felt for his fedora.

"My hat!" he cried. "I've lost my hat. It must've fallen off in the tower."

"Too bad," said Frankie, grinning. "I hope it didn't have magical properties to protect you against evil forces."

"I have to go back for it," Eddie said.

Frankie looked up at the sheer face of the wall.

"Good luck," was all she could say.

"Forget it, Eddie," Walker said. "We don't have the time. We've got to go."

"Okay, my captain," Frankie declared cheerfully. "Lead us on into the darkness and victory!"

"Actually," Walker corrected her, "Eddie's going to have to do the leading since he's the only one who's been to Litherium."

"It's easy," Eddie assured him. "There's only one road and it goes directly from the Kingdom to the city. It's a long way on foot, though."

"I don't think we should take the road," Walker said. "At least not in the beginning. It's the obvious place to look for us and bring us back if that's what Lumina wants to do."

"I doubt she'd do that," replied Eddie. "She's so frantic about not upsetting the Black Count."

"She may think that just us being in Diabolonia would antagonize him enough," Walker said, "and that stopping us would show that she doesn't want to annoy him. Let's not take the risk anyway."

"If we go around it'll be a long walk," Eddie warned him.

"In that case we'd better start right now," Walker replied.

They set off across the rocky ground. It was hard going in the dark and on stones that cut into their sneakers. It was also significantly colder on this side of the walls, and Walker tried to keep up a quick pace, not only to get to Litherium sooner, but also to keep warm.

As they moved farther away from the Kingdom the only light they had to guide them was the glow that their bodies produced and that of Eddie's sword. Walker kept looking over his shoulder back toward Nebula, partly to give himself a sense of the direction they were going in and partly for comfort. Hours later they were in total blackness and the Kingdom was just a faint glow on the horizon.

"I think it's safe enough to go back to the road now," Eddie said. "It'll make the walking a little easier."

Eddie veered to the left with Walker and Frankie closely following. They kept near one another not just for the feeling of safety it gave them but also for the light that they shed. Three children huddled together produced a greater brilliance than if they were spread out. Even so they could only see a few feet in front of them and progress got slower and slower. And the temperature was becoming more and more of an issue. Not only was it much colder the farther they went, but they could no longer walk fast enough to keep warm. Eddie's Red Sox jacket helped him but Walker and Frankie were dressed for a summer afternoon in the Outerworld, and where they were now was anything but that.

"I'm freezing," Frankie complained. "And hungry. How can that be? I'm never hungry in the Kingdom."

"That," said Eddie, "is because you're not in the Kingdom now and you're not getting the energy from the Source that we all get there."

"We should have brought some food, then," she grumbled.

"Frankie!" cried Eddie. "Get real. Have you ever seen food in Nebula? Have you ever seen anyone eat there? We don't need it as long as we have the Source."

"Does that mean I'm going to be starving until we get back?" Frankie asked.

"That's exactly what it means," Eddie assured her.

"Oh well," said Frankie. "I suppose all we can do is suck it up and carry on. I warn you, though, I get mean and angry when I'm hungry."

They continued through the barren landscape. Walker had never seen anywhere as desolate as this. There were no plants, no animals, no hills or valleys, nothing except for an endless, flat wasteland.

"How far to the road, do you think?" he asked.

"It's a ways yet," Eddie replied. "We took a long loop around."

He paused for a while.

"This place used to be beautiful," he continued. "It was all covered in soft green moss, and had hundreds of flowers that sparkled with light. It was warm, smelled wonderful, and there was nowhere you'd rather be than out here. I used to come often with my mom and dad and we'd have huge picnics with lots of friends. Then it all got torn up during the first battle with the Shroud, long before Barren Plains, and after that everything died. People say it wasn't the hooves of the battle unicorns that did it but the evil that flowed from the Black Count and the Shroud. Whatever it was, it's never been the same since."

They continued in silence for a while until Frankie suddenly said, "Eddie, how old are you?"

"How old do you think I am?" Eddie replied.

"Well," said Frankie, "you look about eleven, but you can't be, can you? I mean if you were here with your folks before the battle that was even before the Battle of

Barren Plains, then you must be centuries old."

"It's a long story," Eddie muttered.

"Come on, Eddie," urged Walker. "We've got time."

Eddie paused for a while as if trying to make up his mind.

"I really don't feel like getting into it," he finally said.

"Listen, Eddie, we're your friends," Frankie insisted. "You can trust us, both of us."

There was another silence. Eddie looked distressed, as if conflicting thoughts were clashing inside his head. Then he sighed deeply and began.

"As you know," he started, "I am a prince, and the reason I have that title is my father was the king. His name was Lindanor, and he was the king before Leukos, who was his younger brother."

"You mean King Leukos was your uncle?" asked Walker.

"He was," replied Eddie.

"Why didn't you ever call him uncle?" asked Frankie.

"Because first and foremost he was my king," said Eddie. "Now do you want to hear the story or not? Because if you keep asking questions we'll have passed Litherium before I get to the end."

"Sorry," said Walker. "Keep going."

"My mother, the queen, was a very beautiful woman who my father loved dearly, but she was an Outerworlder," Eddie continued. "There have been Chosen Ones in the Outerworld for many Eons. How they first got there nobody knows, but what we do know is that any Outerworlder with the mark has Nebulite blood somewhere in their ancestry."

"Even me?" asked Walker.

"Even you," Eddie assured him.

"Never mind Walker's ancestry," Frankie said impatiently. "Get on with the story!"

Eddie continued. "My mother loved my father, and they were happiest when they were together, but that wasn't often. In those days it was easy to travel between the Sister Cities, and as the king of Nebula my father had to visit them to sign treaties and perform other official duties. Sometimes my mother went with him, but mostly she was left behind. She became friendly with the Black Count. He was part of Nebula then, and the reason she found him fascinating was that he could do magic. Everyone in the Palace knew he could do tricks— make objects disappear, things like that—but nobody knew how evil his magic really was, not even my mother. The Count loved power—he still does—and he saw my mom as a way of getting it.

"One day, when my father was on one of his journeys, I was playing by myself in the Lightkeepers' chamber. I had made a hidden camp under the throne and was sitting in it when I heard two people come into the room. One was the Black Count, and I still don't know who the other was, because he never said anything. I suspect it was Luzaro—Thoren, that is.

"Anyway, the Count told this other person that he was going to bring my father's reign to an end, marry my mother, the queen, and take power himself. The Count warned the other person that if he mentioned anything of the plot to anyone else, he would kill him, slowly and painfully.

"They left the chamber, not realizing that I was there and heard everything the Count said. I was terrified that if he found out I knew all about the plot he would kill *me* slowly and painfully, so I never said anything to anyone. It was a cowardly thing to do, but I was so scared of the Count.

"When my father returned the Count told him he had discovered a plot to overthrow him and would tell all the details if he would meet him on the ramparts, just the two of them, no guards or servants. My father agreed, but I think he suspected something was up. The Count's plan was to push my father over the wall to his death below and pretend it was an accident, but my father was strong and a good fighter, and in the end it was the Count who was thrown over the parapet, not into Diabolonia, but into a courtyard inside the walls. It was a shorter drop so he wasn't killed, but the impact blinded him.

"My father was a merciful man, and he thought that losing his sight was punishment enough for the Count, but he banished him into the Outer Wastes. As he left the Count swore that as long as he lived he would live only for revenge, and if he was doomed to dwell in darkness he would bring darkness to all the citizens of the Kingdom and every other citadel across the land."

Eddie paused.

"Shortly after this the mark of the Chosen One began to fade from my face," Eddie continued.

"You were a Chosen One?" gasped Walker.

"I was," Eddie assured him, "but I lost the mark many Eons ago because of my secret. When I didn't warn my father I put his life in danger, and because he was the king I put all of Nebula in danger."

"But you were just a kid!" Frankie exclaimed.

"That's true," Eddie agreed, "but I was also a prince,

and from the time I was a young boy I was told that my duty was allegiance to the king and putting the welfare of my people before my own."

"Anyway, how do you know that the mark faded because of your secret?" Walker asked. "Nobody knew you had a secret."

Walker's question made Eddie's mind race back to that terrible day shortly after the mark had faded. His father had just returned from a visit to the Sanctuary, a grim look on his face.

"I have disturbing news to tell you," he said to Eddie, placing his hands on the boy's shoulders. "We all make mistakes," the king continued. "All of us. But yours was a dangerous one because it could have put the whole Kingdom in peril. Because of it the Source has removed your mark, but you have an opportunity to redeem yourself. You will remain a boy and be given the freedom to behave like a boy until you perform an act of bravery that is the true mark of a Chosen One. Until that time you will search the Outerworld for one who can replace you as my heir. This the Source has decreed."

Eddie shook his head to try to expel the memory from his brain. He turned to Walker with a look of intense sadness.

"The Source knew, don't ask me how. Just take my word for it," Eddie said. "The Source gives power, but it can also take it away."

"What happened next?" asked Frankie.

"Nothing was heard of the Count for a long time and life carried on as usual," Eddie told them. "Then there were rumors he had met up with a fearsome tribe of creatures that lived in the farthest parts of the Outer Wastes and had trained them into an army and named them the Warriors of the Black Shroud. Our patrols reported he had already destroyed some of the most distant citadels and that his army was advancing toward Nebula and the Sister Cities.

"My father took his bravest knights and rode out to meet the enemy. The Count and his Warriors were waiting in ambush, and for the first time they used darkning bolts. They weren't as powerful as they are now but they were still good enough to kill my father. I was standing next to him when he died. His unicorn reared up and then they both collapsed to the ground. The sword flew out of my father's hand and landed at my feet. I picked it up and I've carried it with me ever since. It wasn't until King Leukos fought the Battle of Barren Plains with the Lances of Light that the Count was defeated."

"What happened to your mother?" Frankie asked.

"After King Leukos's coronation she returned to the Outerworld, but her life was over, and shortly afterward she died of a broken heart," Eddie answered. "I was left an orphan, and now the kingdom is as well. You are our only hope, for without a king in Nebula we will surely fall."

CHAPTER 20

That is such an awful story!" Frankie exclaimed.

"What happened to you after all this?" Walker asked.

"King Leukos became like my father and protected me," said Eddie. "He was a good man and he became a great king even though he never expected to rule. But he had no children, and since I couldn't be his heir he ordered me to continue the search for a Chosen One. Even though King Leukos carried the mark he was never able to go between the two worlds because he had no Outerworld blood in his veins."

Walker had been so fascinated by Eddie's strange tale that he hadn't noticed they had come to the road and it became a little easier to walk. It still looked like an abandoned highway, but had fewer potholes and rocks. Suddenly Eddie stopped, holding his arms wide to halt Frankie and Walker.

"Do you see what I see?" he asked Walker.

"I do," Walker replied. "There's something out there."

It was difficult to make out in the blackness, but both boys thought they could see tall, towering shapes on either side of the road ahead of them.

"I'll go find out what it is," Walker whispered to Eddie.

"No," said Eddie. "You stay here with Frankie. I'll go. I'm the only one who's armed."

With his sword held out in front of him to light his way Eddie crept forward. The darkness was so intense that he had only gone a few yards before he disappeared completely, and they could do nothing but wait for his return. The only way they knew he was out there at all was the occasional flash of his sword or the sound of stones being dislodged and tumbling down. This went on for some time until suddenly they saw him high above their heads beckoning them over.

"I think we've found Litherium," he called down in a hushed voice. "The only problem is we're too late."

"Why?" Walker called back.

"You'll see soon enough," Eddie replied.

"Is it safe?" Walker asked.

"Yeah, come on over," Eddie said. "But be careful."

They crept cautiously toward the light from Eddie's sword. As they got closer they realized why he was up above their heads. He was standing on the ruins of a wall very similar to the one that surrounded the Kingdom, except that this one had a massive gap in it. They went through the gap, and from the light of their bodies they could just make out the silhouettes of buildings that looked as if giants had trampled on them. Most of the roofs were gone, and many of the walls leaned at crazy angles.

"What do you think happened here?" whispered Frankie.

"I don't know," replied Walker, "and I'm not sure I want to find out."

Eddie had clambered back down the wall and caught up to them.

"You think this is Litherium?" Walker asked him.

"Or what's left of it," said Eddie.

"Who do you think did all this?" asked Frankie.

"It has to be the work of the Black Count and the Shroud," Eddie replied. "There's no one else it can be."

"But where are the people who live here?" asked Frankie.

"Who knows?" Eddie said. "They were probably made into slaves. Either that or . . ." He shrugged his shoulders.

"Yikes," said Frankie.

Walker looked around and a wave of fear and panic flooded over him. How could the peaceful people of Nebula possibly defend themselves against the power that created this destruction? Maybe Lumina was right. Maybe their only hope was to leave the Black Count alone and pray that he would do the same. The awfulness of it seemed to drain away his energy.

"Guys," he said, "I think we should go back."

As he suggested this they heard stones being kicked in the distance. Walker raised his hand.

"There's someone or something out there," he whispered.

"I'll go and see what it is," said Eddie.

"Be careful," Walker warned him.

He ran in the direction of the sound, using the wrecked buildings for cover and the soft glow still radiating from his body to guide him. The silence was suddenly broken by a yell.

"Ow, ow, please, sir, please don't hurt me," said a voice none of them recognized.

"Come with me and let's see who you are," they heard Eddie say.

Moments later Eddie came around the corner of one of the ruins holding a filthy and terrified child by the ear.

"Eddie," Frankie cried out, "she's just a little kid! Let go of her!"

The child in question was no more than four or five. Eddie released his grip as if she was suddenly red-hot.

"Well, how was I to know?" he protested. "It's dark out there and she might have been dangerous."

In all his life Walker had never seen anyone who looked less dangerous.

"Come, sit down," he said, gently. "It's okay. We won't hurt you."

The girl sat on the stone Walker pointed to. Her eyes were wide and her body was shaking.

"Tell me," he continued, "what is the name of this place?"

"It's called Litherium," she replied, her lower lip quivering and her eyes filling with tears.

"And what happened here?" Walker asked.

She began to reply but could hold back her tears no longer, and sobbed as if she would sob forever. Frankie put her arms around her.

"You don't have to tell us now," she assured her. "What's your name?"

The girl lifted up her tear-streaked face.

"It's Ferna," she replied.

"I'm pleased to meet you, Ferna," Frankie said. "My name's Frankie, and this is Walker and Eddie and we're from Nebula. We came here to ask for Litherium's help."

"There's no one here who can help you," said Ferna. "There's only me and the rest of the children."

"The rest of the children?" asked Walker.

"They're in one of the smashed-up houses over there," she said, pointing. "When we heard you coming I snuck out to see if they'd come back."

"To see if who'd come back?" said Walker.

"Them monster things," she replied.

Then she told the story of what had happened. The city had been peacefully going about its business when the temperature suddenly dropped, and howling winds began to blow through the streets. The earth started to shake, darkning bolts rained down, and then they saw the Warriors of the Black Shroud.

"They were huge monsters," Ferna said. "They stepped on the walls and on the houses and crushed them like they were nothing. Then they began to push everyone into the town square, and anyone who tried to get away was hit with them darkning things. When everyone was in the square they smashed down the Town Hall and put out the Sacred Flame and everywhere went dark, but they didn't care because they can't see anyway."

"What is—was--the Sacred Flame?" asked Walker.

"It's a flame that burns forever, least that's what I was told," Ferna explained. "It was where we got all our fire from. Without fire we have no light, and no heat, no food—nothing."

"Food?" exclaimed Frankie. "You eat fire?"

"Of course," replied Ferna. "What else would you eat?"

"Didn't you try to fight back?" Eddie finally asked.

"The archers fired flaming arrows at the monsters but they all just bounced off," Ferna said.

"How did you escape?" Walker asked.

"When they were getting everyone in the square," she replied, "my dad took my mom in one hand and me in the other and we ran as fast as we could go. I thought we were going to make it but those dark things hit my mom and dad and they just vanished . . ."

Once again she broke down into uncontrollable sobs, and they had to wait for these to let up before she could continue.

"I don't know why," she said when she was able, "but I was left standing by myself, and the monsters didn't seem to know I was there. I just waited until they took everyone off into Diabolonia. I thought I was alone and then I heard one of the other kids, and then another and another. I think they're all here. Why they didn't take us I don't know."

"It looks like you were right," Eddie said to Walker.

"Do you have any fire?" Ferna asked. "If we don't eat soon we're all going to die."

"No," said Walker, "but don't worry. We'll bring you back to Nebula and you'll have everything you need. Now, take us to the other children."

"Please don't hurt them," she begged.

"You can trust us," he said. "We won't harm them. Besides, there are probably more of you than us, so I should be begging *you* not to hurt *us*."

The exhausted child tried to smile, and she almost did.

With Ferna leading they made their way down ruined, rubble-strewn streets. She stopped in front of a house that wasn't as badly damaged as the others.

"They're in here," she said, "but let me go first and tell them who you are."

She paused.

"What shall I tell them?" she asked, confused.

"Tell them that we're friends from Nebula," Frankie advised her.

Ferna disappeared inside the house and Walker, Frankie, and Eddie could hear the sound of children talking in hushed tones. Then they heard Ferna shout out.

"Okay. Come on in."

Despite Ferna's reassurance the children were terrified to see three glowing strangers, one holding a shining sword. They had been in total darkness for so long that the light was too much for them and they had to shade their eyes. It was hard to tell how many children were there. Walker thought there had to be at least sixty, but probably more.

"Don't worry, everybody," Walker addressed them. "We're your friends and we'll get you back to Nebula. That's where we come from, and it's safe there. The creatures that attacked Litherium will never be able to attack Nebula because we have a thing called the Source and it gives us energy and light and it's too powerful for our enemies to destroy." Walker hoped that what he was telling the children was true.

"That's what they said about the Sacred Flame," protested one of the children.

"Well, the Source really is," Walker said, "and we'll start back there soon."

Walker felt Eddie tugging on his sleeve.

"We need to talk," Eddie muttered. "And not here."

Reassuring the children that they would be back in a short time, Walker, Eddie, and Frankie went outside the house and back into the street.

"What's up?" Walker asked Eddie.

"We can't take these kids back to Nebula—well, not yet at least," Eddie replied. "Our mission wasn't just to find Litherium, but to get help to defend the Kingdom. Since there's no help here, we have to move on."

"To where?" asked Walker.

"There are other Sister Cities out there and they may still be all right," Eddie said. "We have to find the nearest one. If we go back to Nebula with the children Lumina will put us away somewhere and our last chance to get help will be gone."

"Do you know where the nearest Sister City is?" asked Frankie.

"Well, no," admitted Eddie, "but it's somewhere out there."

"There's a lot of 'out there' out there," Frankie pointed out, "and these kids need to get to safety. I say we take them back to Nebula now."

"But don't you see," said Eddie in frustration, "if we go back Lumina will never let us or anyone else go for help, and the Kingdom will be doomed."

"I think you're wrong, Eddie, and I'll tell you why," Walker said. "I think the kids will be the best way of convincing her of the threat from the Black Count, and that he isn't just going to leave us alone. Once we've told her about Litherium and she's heard the kids' stories there's no way she can pretend that everything's all right."

"You don't know her as well as I do," Eddie assured him. "She's stubborn, that one."

"You're right, I don't know her as well as you do," Walker agreed. "But I do know we have to get these children to safety. We can't just leave them here. It's a risk we have to take."

Eddie sighed.

"I suppose you're right," he said.

"Okay, then," said Walker. "Let's get them ready to go."

They began to walk back to the house when they

suddenly felt a slight rumbling in the ground beneath their feet, almost as if a truck had passed nearby. Eddie looked up and cocked his head like a dog.

"Did you feel that?" he asked.

Before anyone could answer him the vibrations came again, only stronger than before, and the air suddenly turned cold. They ran back into the house to find the children confused and frightened. Frankie grabbed Walker's hand, and everyone instinctively huddled together.

"It's them!" a child cried. "They're coming back! They've come back to get us!"

"What're we going to do?" asked Frankie.

"Don't worry," Walker said, "I'll think of something."

CHAPTER 21

The rumbling of the earth got louder, and the vibrations sent cascades of rocks tumbling from the ruined walls. Suddenly the shaking stopped, and all that could be heard was the sound of deep, heavy breathing, interspersed with snorting and grunting. Then there was a roar, and a flash of blackness followed by a crashing sound as one of the last remaining walls of an already-ruined house came tumbling to the ground behind them.

"That was a darkning bolt," whispered Eddie to Walker.

Walker looked at the house they were in. Although it was in better shape than the others on the street, it was still heavily damaged. Half the roof was missing, and if a darkning bolt even came close to it there was the real danger of collapse. Everyone inside would be trapped.

"We've got to get these kids out of here," he decided.

"Better get them close to the city walls," Eddie said. "They're not much protection but they're thicker and sturdier than any of the houses."

Walker remembered the huge hole in the fortifications that they had scrambled through, but he hadn't seen anything that looked safer and so they gathered the children together and led them to the foot of the wall, telling them to stay pressed up against the stone and away from the open space. Then a voice sounded out of the blackness, deep, booming, and petrifying.

"Children!" the Black Count shouted. "We know you're there. Come outside of the walls and we will take you to your parents. They miss you and are waiting for you."

"It's the Black Count," whispered Eddie. "Nobody has a voice like his."

"If they can't see us, how do they know we're here?" asked Frankie.

There was no time to answer her. A line of children was already making its way to the gap in the walls.

"No!" yelled Walker. "Stop. It's a trick so that they can capture you as well. Stay here."

"Don't go!" cried Eddie. "This is the same man that destroyed your homes and captured your parents. Don't trust him. He's evil."

The Black Count roared again, and in doing so answered Frankie's question.

"Don't listen to those boys," he thundered. "One is an Outerworlder, an intruder who doesn't know our ways, and the other is a treacherous child and a coward. Come out into open ground and sing a song so that my warriors know where you are and can take you back to your parents and safety."

One of the children started to sing in a voice quavering with fear. Frankie went up to him and softly put two of her fingers against his lips.

"Shhh," she said gently and quietly. "Don't make a sound. If they can't hear you they don't know where you are. Eddie's right. That man is evil. He has taken your parents away from you, but we know good people, brave people in Nebula, and they will come and rescue them."

The children were confused, not knowing what to do.

Then one of the boys leaped to his feet and scrambled to the top of the damaged wall.

"You send our parents back here!" he yelled, anger making his voice shake. "You smashed my house and left me in darkness and now I don't have anywhere to live and I don't have my parents and my sister's scared and I hate you!"

He picked up a rock and hurled it in the direction of the voice. The fear and tension that had overwhelmed the children broke, and the others ran and joined the boy on the wall, picking up rocks as they did. Soon the ramparts were lined with children all throwing stones high into the darkness and yelling at the top of their lungs. Then they heard the Black Count's voice again, bellowing in fury.

"You foolish children!" roared the Count. "Do you think you can fight the Warriors of the Black Shroud?"

Darkning bolts started coming thick and fast. At first they seemed as poorly aimed as the one that hit the house, but then they began to come closer to the stone throwers.

"Oh no!" cried Walker. "We have to stop them. The warriors can't make out where the kids are, but they're aiming for the stones."

No sooner had he said this than one of the bolts found its mark. It struck the boy who had started the stone throwing; he simply disappeared. Ferna, who had stayed close to Frankie the entire time, let out a terrifying cry.

"Lathan, come back!" she screamed. "Don't take my brother. Please don't take my brother."

Walker and Eddie ran toward the remaining children.

"Stop throwing the stones!" Walker yelled at the top of his lungs.

"Come back! Come back!" cried Eddie.

It was no use. The children either couldn't hear them over the sound of their own shouting, or they simply couldn't stop once they had started. But when they saw two more of their friends struck and vanished, they began to panic. One boy jumped from the wall, landed badly, and lay unconscious on the ground. The others didn't seem to know which way to turn. Although they had stopped throwing the telltale stones, the Warriors now knew where to target and they continued to hurl down the terrifying bolts.

Walker and Eddie climbed to the top of the wall. Eddie scrambled up the debris and got there first. One by one he guided the children down, shielding them with his body as darkning bolts crashed around them. Walker was helping only a few feet behind when a succession of bolts smashed into the masonry by Eddie's feet.

"Stop! Just stop!" Eddie yelled, brandishing his sword above his head in fury.

Another bolt came flying out of the darkness and hit the weapon, pulling it out of Eddie's hand and sending it flying through the air. It came to rest in the pile of masonry near the gap in the wall, only just missing several of the terrified children. Eddie stood on top of the wall, dazed and unarmed. For a brief moment there was silence, followed by one more shaft of blackness that hurtled toward him and struck him full in the face. And then he was gone.

Walker felt himself shaking with anger. He grabbed the sword and scrambled to the top of the wall, where he stood holding it in both hands.

"No, no, no!" he cried. "He was my friend. You've taken my friend."

This produced another barrage of bolts, barely missing Walker. One came right at his face, and in panic Walker instinctively swung Eddie's sword at it as if it were a baseball bat. To his astonishment the bolt glanced off the blade and flew back into the darkness. His hands tingled from the force of the contact and his body felt like a giant fist had punched it—but he was still there.

"Come down! Please come down!" yelled Frankie.

As it turned out, Walker didn't have any choice in the matter. One of the bolts destroyed the part of the wall he was standing on, taking out a large chunk and causing him to tumble to the ground several feet below. He landed with a thump that knocked all the wind out of his body. Frankie raced over to him.

"Walker! Are you all right?" she cried. "Can you hear me? Can you move your arms and legs?"

Walker sat up and shook his head, trying to get rid of the dazed feeling. He looked at Frankie.

"Yeah, I think I'm okay," he reassured her. "Help me up."

She grabbed his hand and pulled him to his feet. He peered around in the gloom. The remaining children were huddled together against the wall. The boy who had jumped had regained consciousness, but was lying down, his leg swollen and obviously causing him pain.

"Please," he said to Walker. "I don't feel good. Can you get us out of here?"

There was a lull in the attack and everything was quiet. Walker looked at the huddled group of children. Each one of them was relying upon him to save them and he had no idea how. How could he rescue all those faces turned toward him, waiting for his next move?

Suddenly another torrent of darkning bolts rained down on the wall and a large part of it broke away and crashed to the ground. Beneath the rubble Walker could see the blade of the sword that had tumbled from his hands when he fell. He went over to where it lay, carefully pulled the debris away, and lifted up the gleaming weapon. He looked at the intricate workings of the blade through a blur of tears. Eddie was gone and all that was left of him was this weapon and an ache inside that Walker had never felt before.

His hands tightened around the handle of the sword. Eddie had died heroically protecting the children, and now Walker owed it to him to keep them safe. He ran back to the wall and slowly moved up to where it had collapsed. Cautiously he looked out into Diabolonia, but the darkness was so dense that he could see nothing. He brought the sword around and by its light he could just make out the monstrous silhouettes of some Warriors of the Black Shroud. They stood motionless, as if awaiting orders from the Black Count, who was nowhere to be seen.

Frankie sidled up next to him.

"How many can you see?" she whispered.

"Not many, but boy, they're big!" he replied quietly.

"What should we do?" said Frankie.

"We've got to get the children back to Nebula," Walker told her. "If we don't escape soon we're either going to be captured by the Shroud or killed by a falling building."

"But it's miles and miles and miles to Nebula," she protested. "It took us forever, and don't forget we've got that boy with the injured leg."

"You're just going to have to do the best you can," he muttered.

"What do you mean 'you're going to have to do the best you can'?" cried Frankie in a loud voice.

"Shhh," whispered Walker. "Don't let them hear us. You're going to have to lead the kids back to the Kingdom. You know the way as well as I do."

"And what will you be doing?" she asked, only quietly this time.

"I'm going to try and distract the Shroud," he replied. "As far as I can see there's only about four or five of them, and we know they can hear us so I'm going to go out there and start yelling at them, calling them names, and things like that. They're bound to come after me, and that'll give you and the others the chance to get away."

"Walker Watson, you can't possibly do that," Frankie hissed. "You'll never get away with it. They'll get you in a heartbeat."

"I doubt it," said Walker. "With their size I'd be surprised if they can move as fast as I can. Besides which, I've got the sword if things get really hairy."

"That's nuts," snorted Frankie under her breath.

"Do you have a better plan?" Walker asked.

"No," Frankie admitted, "but that doesn't make yours a good one."

"In that case I'm going to stick with mine," he said.

Before she could say anything else he leaped through the gap in the wall and ran toward the nearest Warrior. When he looked up at the sightless giant that loomed over him, he almost ran back, but his nerve held. He took a deep breath and then yelled.

"Hey, you overgrown piece of dirt, you think you can make a slave of me? You think you can even come near me? You're so slow you couldn't catch me if I was running on one leg."

The monster turned toward the sound of his voice. With every step it took, the ground shuddered beneath its weight. It began to move slowly toward him. Walker looked to his right and saw another not too far away. If he could get that one to come toward him maybe they would crash into each other. Maybe he could get them to destroy each other. He ran toward it.

"You may be bigger than me," he shouted, "but you're so stooopid! And did I mention ugly? Well, you are!"

Sure enough, the second one began to move in his direction. He ran to one side to watch the two creatures slowly close in on each other, but just when it seemed inevitable that they would collide some instinct kicked in and they both turned toward him. He ran in the opposite direction of Litherium, hoping to draw them away long enough to give Frankie the opportunity to escape with the children. But instead of drawing them away he was running into more of them. Suddenly he realized that what he had thought to be only four or five Warriors was actually dozens, maybe hundreds of the creatures. He was surrounded by them.

There was nothing for it but to run back toward the comparative safety of the city, and hope that Frankie hadn't tried to make it out with the children. He dodged and weaved through the enemy, at one point actually running between the legs of one. Finally he made it through the lurching hulks and there was open space between him and Litherium. He was almost at the walls when the darkning bolts began. At first there were just one or two, but slowly they began to get closer, and he just got to the outer perimeter when a furious fusillade of bolts came crashing down. He threw himself over the rubble where the wall had collapsed and rolled over and over until he was behind the protection of the part that was still standing.

"Just four or five of them did that?"

To his immense relief Frankie was standing there, huddled against the wall with the children. They all looked shaken but okay apart from that.

"No, apparently I didn't see them all," admitted Walker.

"That's good," said Frankie, "because if that's the work of just four or five we'll never get out of here."

As more bolts rained down it occurred to Walker for the first time that it was likely they wouldn't.

"What's plan B?" asked Frankie.

"Your guess is as good as mine," he admitted.

"Uh-oh, that's not good news," she said. "Because I don't have a clue what we should do."

They stared at each other, their fear clearly showing on their faces. Then a thought struck Walker that caused his expression to change. It was a memory that gradually cleared in his mind like a picture coming into focus.

"Oh, Power of the Source, I command you to come to the aid of a Chosen One as is your ancient duty and pledge," he said softly under his breath, almost like a prayer.

"What did you say?" asked Frankie.

"It's something I remembered the king telling me," Walker told her. "I don't know if it'll make any difference."

At first nothing happened except that the constant stream of black streaks bursting from the Warriors stopped for a moment, but this was to be short-lived. A roar came from the Black Count.

"You are beyond help, Chosen One," he bellowed. "Your mark cannot protect you here, and you will be our prized captive. When we enter the Kingdom you will lead us through its gates in chains. *That* is your destiny; for *that* you have been chosen!"

The barrage resumed with more ferocity than before, and the bolts kept coming closer. One landed just a few feet from them, causing everything to shake and sucking up dust and rubble from all directions, but the walls held firm. Frankie pushed as close to Walker as she could.

"I'm sorry I brought you here," Walker said to her. "I never should've."

"I made you bring me here," Frankie reassured him. "I wanted to see the Kingdom, and I'm glad I did because it's a really cool place. We just tried to do stuff we probably should have left to grown-ups."

"Well, we did get through when they couldn't," he reminded her. "Not that it did us much good. I suppose I started to believe that I really was a Chosen One and that nothing bad could ever happen to me."

"It's scary to think we may never see our parents or the Outerworld again," Frankie said. "With that time-difference thing, do you think they'll even know we're gone?" And at that point she did a very un-Frankielike thing. She began to cry.

Then Walker did a very un-Walkerlike thing. He put his arms around her to comfort her, and holding on to each other they waited for whatever was going to be their fate. He felt Frankie's sobs shake her body, but as they huddled together he was suddenly aware of a strange light coming from the other side of the wall like the very beginning of dawn, and he could hear a low humming sound.

"Something's happening!" he cried. "Something that

has to be good, 'cause there's light. Stay there, every-body. I'm going to go see."

"Not without me, you're not," Frankie declared, and she grasped his hand firmly.

Not even bothering to argue, he cautiously led her along to where the wall had collapsed. They gingerly peered out, and what they saw was the most amazing sight either of them had ever seen.

CHAPTER 22

Is it true what this page tells me?" thundered Lumina. "Did you allow those foolish children to go by themselves into Diabolonia?"

Jevon looked her squarely in the eye.

"Those very brave children went into Diabolonia to make contact with the citizens of Litherium," he told her.

Astrodor was standing to one side of Lumina. He looked uncomfortable now that Jevon knew he was the informer. When Jevon had been taken to the Chamber of the Lightkeepers, he had expected to confront Lumina and the others immediately, but this had not been the case. He'd been kept waiting in the adjacent hallway for a long time, always in the presence of two knights. Although he wasn't handcuffed or shackled, it was clear to him that he wasn't free to leave, and he waited as patiently as he could until he was finally brought in front of Lumina. She was seated on the old king's throne and she was not happy.

"Not only was this against my specific command," she continued, glowering at him, "but children, Jevon! You allowed children to do this! Have you lost your mind?"

"No, my lady," he replied. "On the contrary, my mind tells me that it's likely the Warriors of the Black Shroud are incapable of identifying targets as small as children and because of this they have the best chance of reaching Litherium unharmed. It is vital for the survival of this Kingdom that we join with the citizens of the Sister Cities to defend ourselves against the Black Count, because I am convinced that there is no peace to be had with him."

Lumina got up from the throne and walked over to the nearest window. She stood there looking out over the Kingdom and then turned to face Jevon.

"My lord," she said, "I pray that you are wrong. My greatest hope is that we can come to an agreement with the Black Count that meets both our needs."

She paused for a moment.

"I look at you, Lord Jevon," she continued, "and all the other fine young Lightkeepers assembled here, and I have to remind myself that I am the only one left in the Kingdom who has ever known war and its horrors. They called me the Warrior Princess even though I was not of royal blood and never carried the mark. I earned this title because there was no fight so fearsome, no skirmish so brutal that could make me back away. But after the Battle of Barren Plains, which the Book of the Kingdom will tell you was a great victory, I vowed I would do everything in my power to make sure that no mothers mourned daughters, no wives lost husbands, no brothers wept over brothers because of me."

All eyes were upon Lumina with one exception: A knight standing next to a window suddenly cried out, breaking the silence that descended when she finished speaking.

"My lady!" the knight cried. "Something very strange is happening!"

Everyone rushed to the windows and stood open-mouthed.

"What's going on?" someone asked.

Lumina looked out of the window and then turned to Jevon.

"Lord Jevon," Lumina said with a troubled look on her face. "I fear your children are in extreme danger. The Chosen One has summoned what you see before you. He has invoked an ancient command that only works in times of utmost peril."

"If this is true, my lady, then we must go to their aid with all speed!" cried Jevon. "Allow me to lead as many knights as will join me to rescue them."

Lumina sighed.

"Go, my lord," she said, "and may your mission be successful. Save those foolish children."

The first thing Walker and Frankie saw as they peered out into Diabolonia was a glow of light some distance away, but they couldn't make out where it came from. All they knew was that it was getting closer, and the humming sound that accompanied it was getting louder. This was almost drowned out by the only other noise they could hear—a roaring, both angry and fearful, that came from the direction of the Warriors.

Walker realized that the bombardment of darkning

bolts had stopped, and this had given him the courage to move into the open to get a better view. Then he could make out what it was that shed the life-giving light. He could see birds—hundreds, no, probably thousands of birds. They were the same ones that drifted on the air currents above the Kingdom, but now they drifted no more. They were in a tight V formation, a vast glowing triangle, and they were led by a creature much larger than they were.

"I cannot believe my eyes," whispered Frankie in awe.

When Walker had spoken the Ancient Cry of Peril, every animal in the Kingdom, every bird circling above, every dragon below, all the creatures within the walls had felt impelled to come to his assistance. As the knights who had joined Jevon in the rescue mission rushed to their unicorns, they found them pulling against the reins that tethered them as they tried to break free and gallop to the Chosen One's assistance. Walker's own unicorn, Lightning, had done what only a Silverstreak of the king's herd was able to do. She'd spread the wings that until now had lain hidden behind her shoulders, and with a whooshing sound she took to the air. It was Lightning that Walker and Frankie saw now, leading the enormous flock of silver birds. She spotted the two friends by the wall and started to spiral down. She landed beside them and folded her wings back into her body. Walker threw his arms around her neck.

"Lightning, you came to rescue us!" he yelled. "You are the most wonderful unicorn in the Kingdom."

Lightning pawed the ground with her hooves and blew through her nostrils as if in agreement. The birds she had been leading had not landed with her, but had continued on their flight path. Walker and Frankie turned to watch along with the children, and what they saw they would remember for as long as they lived.

The Warriors of the Black Shroud had assembled in lines that went on as far as the eye could see. Walker gasped when he saw how many of them there were, but the birds flew calmly on. As they reached their targets they wheeled down, circling each Warrior, flying so close that their silver wings brushed against them.

On the ground dogs, dragons, and strange little furry creatures Walker hadn't seen before ran fearlessly toward the Warriors. The dragons blew clouds of light from their nostrils while the little creatures that looked like a cross between a rat and a hamster swarmed up the enemy's legs as the dogs nipped at the Warriors' ankles.

The monsters began to stumble around, banging into

one another, unable to find a way to escape. It was as if the light from the birds and animals actually caused them pain. Deafening claps of thunder crashed above their heads, and in a vain attempt to defend themselves some tried to shield their sightless faces with their arms, while others pointed their fingers toward the attackers, but the shafts of darkness they shot out evaporated as they struck the radiance of the massive flock of birds.

Then one by one the Warriors began to disappear in exactly the same way that Eddie had disappeared. They just vanished, leaving no trace, no hood, no cape, nothing. It was as if they had never existed. Many fell in the chaos that ensued, giving the animals and birds the chance to swoop down on their sprawling bodies. Those who did get away ran as fast as they could. It was amazing to see such huge creatures fleeing for their lives, and despite what Walker had thought, they moved with incredible speed and were gone. Only one was left, the largest and most fearsome of the Shroud. In front of him stood the Black Count, turning his sightless head from side to side as he realized the disaster unfolding around him.

"Come back, you cowards!" he roared. "Obey your master now!"

But none did, and the remaining Warrior bent down

and picked him up like a baby, and he, too, ran into the farthest depths of Diabolonia.

"That was awesome," whispered Frankie.

When the last Warrior disappeared all that was left was an empty, barren landscape illuminated by the birds' wings. The surviving children jumped up and down with excitement, and then Walker noticed them looking up into the sky. He followed their eyes to see what the birds were doing now.

The main body was heading home, but two groups had peeled off. One now hovered over their heads, while another, larger formation flew in the opposite direction, away from the Kingdom. Frankie saw it too.

"Where do you think they're going?" she asked.

"I don't know," answered Walker, "but I think I'm going there too."

Lightning whinnied and dropped to her knees, waiting to be mounted. He leapt on her back and began to urge her forward.

"Hey!" cried Frankie. "Not without me!"

"You stay with the children and get them back to Nebula," he told her.

"You're going to leave me all alone?" she yelled.

"All alone?" Walker snorted. "Look around you,

Frankie. You've never been less alone in your whole life."

He was right. Now that the enemy had fled, several of the animals had gathered around the delighted children. Frankie was surrounded by the strange little furry creatures, several dogs, and two small dragons. One of the birds had landed on her shoulder.

"I'll see you back in the Kingdom!" he shouted as Lightning moved forward.

"Walker Watson!" Frankie cried out. "That is so totally not cool to leave without me! I'll get you back for that, you see if I don't."

Walker's only response was to wave at her and smile as Lightning began to gather speed.

"Follow the birds," he told the unicorn.

She had no saddle or reins, so he had to hang on to her mane with one hand while he gripped Eddie's sword with the other. Faster and faster she went, until suddenly her wings unfolded with a wumping sound and they were airborne. Walker could feel the beat of her massive wings as they went higher and higher, and then he saw the birds ahead of them.

Lightning quickly caught up with the birds and they regrouped to fly in formation behind the speeding unicorn. They were so close, Walker could make out their every detail. They had alert eyes like a hawk's, but without the sharp, hooked beak. Their feathers looked as if they had been beaten out of thin metal and then polished to a mirror finish. They seemed delicate but strong, graceful yet powerful.

The unicorn and the birds began to lose height and by the light they shed Walker could make out the reason for their descent. Below them was a line of men and women, all going in the same direction that the Shroud had fled. They stumbled forward, their feet shackled, and on either side of the column were Nightangels with whips. They cracked them in the air before bringing them down on the shoulders and legs of their prisoners as they tried to drive them faster into the Outer Wastes. Then Walker saw something that filled his heart with joy and fear at the same time.

At the head of the column were two Warriors of the Black Shroud and several Nightangels armed with spears forged out of black metal. They were guarding one special prisoner—Eddie.

The Nightangels were aware of the birds above their heads and urged their captives on even more harshly. With Walker hanging on for dear life, Lightning swooped down on the Warrior guards. This time the

Warriors' aim was true, and darkning bolts flew within inches of Walker's face, but there was no sucking sensation, and the noise the bolts made was different. A scary thought occurred to Walker—maybe now the Shroud were shooting to kill, not capture.

Lightning ducked and weaved with amazing skill, avoiding the bolts often by a hair's breadth, and almost tossing Walker from her back several times. She flew so close to one of the Warriors that Walker almost brushed against him and would have done so but for the fact that her light caused the monster to reel back. She wheeled around and once again Walker nearly fell off. He thrust out the arm that carried the sword to balance himself and he heard a roar come from the Warrior. The sword had sliced through the creature's shoulder, but there had been no jarring sensation when it did—in fact, no sensation at all. But as he saw the blade penetrate the Warrior's body, its glow of light spread like fire, and the beast began to crumple before disappearing in a cloud of dust.

The other Warrior, sensing its partner's fate, lumbered toward them. Lightning flew straight up until she was high above its head and then plummeted down. She tried to get behind the enemy, away from the deadly bolts, but the monster swung around and Walker looked straight into its featureless metallic face. Walker knew what he had to do. He rammed the sword into its head, and there was a groan from the Warrior, followed by a shower of dust cascading to the ground.

Lightning landed and folded her wings back into her body. The Warrior guards were no more, but the Nightangels were still a threat, and they began to charge, their spears lowered. Walker leaped from Lightning's back.

"Keep them away from me while I free Eddie!" he cried.

Lightning pawed the ground and then let out a long, loud whinny. At the sound of it the birds that had been hovering overhead swooped down and flew among the Nightangels. The birds had talons and sharp beaks with which to fight, and they attacked mercilessly. Lightning used her stubby horn to butt each Nightangel that charged at Walker, or sent them sprawling with a kick from her strong hind legs. This allowed Walker to weave his way through to Eddie until he was face-to-face with his friend.

"Quick, get me free!" Eddie said, holding out his bound wrists. They were fastened together with a thick rope that was easy for the sword to cut through, but the shackles around his ankles were another matter. They were made of the same black metal that formed the Nightangels' spears and there was no way that Eddie's sword would be able to cut through them. As Walker was bent over trying to see how they were fastened, Eddie suddenly yelled out.

"Look out! Behind you!"

Walker swiveled around to see that one of the Night-angels had evaded Lightning and was running at them full tilt. Instinctively Walker raised the sword to defend himself and it made contact with the enemy's spear. This time he felt the blow, and a jarring sensation rippled through his body. He had deflected the Nightangel's stroke, but only for a moment, and already his opponent was preparing himself to make another thrust. Walker tried to get up, but stumbled and fell.

"Quick, throw me the sword!" yelled Eddie.

Walker threw the weapon toward Eddie, who deftly caught it by its handle. Eddie then shuffled toward the Nightangel, beating back each stab of the spear. His skill with the sword was one that had obviously been perfected over many years.

Walker was back on his feet. He looked around to see how he could help his friend. Now that Eddie had the sword, Walker was unarmed—except, of course, for Lightning. She was proving herself to be every bit as good as a sword.

"Lightning, come here, girl!" Walker yelled.

She galloped over to him and he leaped on her back. Since she was his only weapon, he would use her well. He turned her head toward the nearest Nightangel. Then, in the same way he told the unicorn where to go just by thinking of it, he concentrated really hard and conjured up in his mind's eye a picture of Lightning sending the Nightangel flying through the air with her hooves. He felt a bump, heard a cry, and to his delight saw that his vision had come true. The Nightangel lay sprawled on the ground some distance away. It scrambled to its feet and fled.

Walker focused on one enemy after another until the only one left was the creature fighting a desperate duel with Eddie. Walker headed Lightning to where the battle was taking place, only this time he didn't have to imagine the action. Lightning knew exactly what to do. She reared up and then turned her hindquarters to Eddie's opponent and let out a powerful kick with both legs. One hoof hit the Nightangel in the head and another in the chest, and he fell to the ground unconscious.

"Way to go, Lightning!" Walker cried. He leaped from Lightning's back and ran over to Eddie.

"Are you all right?" he asked.

"Yes, I'm fine," Eddie said, trying to catch his breath. "Thanks for the rescue. It took a lot of guts to do that by yourself."

"I wasn't by myself," said Walker, his arm around Lightning's neck.

"No, I suppose not," Eddie agreed. "And you're not going to be by yourself now." He pointed. "Here comes the cavalry!"

Walker looked and saw a cloud of dust and light speeding toward them. As it got closer he began to make out knights on unicorns, their gleaming lances topped with fluttering pennants. King Leukos's jet-black war unicorn led the group, with Jevon mounted on him—and a passenger. Clinging on with one arm and waving with the other was Frankie. As the huge beast thundered to a halt in front of them, she leaped from its back.

"Eddie!" she cried in delight. "Is that you? It is you. It really is!"

CHAPTER 23

Frankie ran toward Eddie. She leaped into the air, wrapping her arms around his neck and her legs around his waist.

"Whoa!" he cried. "You'll have us both on the floor, and I wouldn't want to mess up my best clothes."

The action had happened so quickly that Walker hadn't really looked at everything around him. Eddie's clothes were in fact torn and filthy, with what appeared to be scorch marks on them in several places. But if he was looking disheveled, the people behind him were worse. Their clothes and hair were caked with mud, and beneath the grime their faces looked gray, unhealthy, and exhausted.

"We thought you were dead," said Walker.

"Yes," agreed Eddie. "For the moment so did I. But the Warriors had other plans for me. I was held as a hostage to force the Kingdom to surrender. You, too, I might add, when they got you."

"I'm so glad you're not dead!" squealed Frankie. "I'm not talking to you, Walker Watson," she said, turning to Walker. "How you can call yourself my friend and leave me behind like that I'll never know. Just as well for you Jevon came along when he did, so don't think in the future you can get away from me because as you can see you can't."

"I thought you weren't talking to me," said Walker.

"I'm not," Frankie assured him. "I'm just telling you what you need to know."

Jevon, who was listening to all this, chuckled.

"It's good to see you alive, your royal highness," he said to Eddie. "But what happened to you?"

"I was on top of the wall and got hit by a darkning bolt, and everything went black," Eddie explained. "Then the next thing I knew I was on the ground being guarded by someone or something with whips. Every time I tried to move I got a lash or a poke with a whip handle. And I could hear the sound of digging, lots of people digging, and more whippings and shouts from guards. These poor folk were the diggers, although what they were digging I have no idea."

"Who are they?" whispered Frankie.

"They were prisoners of the Warriors. They lived in the Sister Cities before the invasion of the Black Count," Eddie told her.

Walker noticed that Jevon was standing in front of one of the freed slaves, a man who looked very old and worn-out.

"My lord Valoris—is that you?" he heard the knight ask.

The old man raised his head, and then beneath the grime that caked his face a look of recognition appeared.

"Lord Jevon, my friend." He smiled. "I never thought I would see you again. Did the king lead this rescue?"

"No, my lord," replied Jevon. "He was killed when you were taken prisoner."

Valoris slumped as if someone had hit him.

"I wish I had died there with him and not been captured by these monsters!" he cried.

"Don't say that, my lord. Nebula needs your wisdom and experience now more than ever," Jevon assured him. "Are the rest of the king's patrol here also?"

"They are in this crowd somewhere," Valoris replied. "They separated us when we were first captured."

"Let's see if we can get you and these poor people out of those shackles," said Jevon.

There was a groan from the fallen Nightangel. He had regained consciousness and rolled over.

"Look!" cried Walker. "On his belt—there's a huge bunch of keys."

Two knights ran over and each grabbed one of the Nightangel's arms. When it was clear he couldn't escape, Walker pulled the large metal ring from his belt and gave it to Jevon. There were dozens of keys on it and it took some time to find the right one, but eventually they heard a satisfying click and the metal band fell away from Eddie's ankle.

"Great," said Jevon. "Now let's free the others."

They started the long process of releasing all of the former slaves one by one. As their chains came off they rubbed their wrists and ankles, unsure of what would happen next.

"Master," one of the women said to Jevon, "what do

you want us to do? Where shall we go?"

"I'm not your master," Jevon replied, "for once again you're a free woman. We will take you back to Nebula until you've recovered enough to return to your homes."

"Our homes," she said. "I fear we have no homes."

One of the men, tall and dignified even in his threadbare clothes, turned to Jevon.

"My lord," he said. "My name is Gallimor and I am the leader of those taken from Litherium. Can you tell me, please, if you have any news of our children?"

"Good news," Jevon assured him. "They are all safe and my men are taking them to Nebula as we speak. They were saved by three of our children, who showed much courage."

"We are indebted to these children," Gallimor said, "and long to be reunited with our own."

"As you shall be, and soon," said Jevon. "Lightkeepers— help these people back to the Kingdom."

The knights began to gently organize the former prisoners and slowly started to move them in the direction of Nebula for the long march back. The Nightangel felled by Lightning's hooves was chained in the shackles that Eddie had worn and was prodded to the end of the long line of people.

Jevon turned to the three friends.

"Each of you is as brave as any knight here," he said. "You are all the children of light. King Leukos would have been so proud of you. And your father," he said to Eddie, "would have been so pleased to know what a brave son he had."

"Is the Black Count finally defeated?" Walker asked. "Or will he and the Shroud try again?"

"I wish we had been able to get here sooner," answered Jevon. "Then maybe we would have had total victory over the Count. But yes, he will return. Evil like his does not vanish of its own accord; it must be vanquished. Now we must get you and these poor folk back to the Kingdom."

Jevon gave the command to the knights to mount up. When they were back on their unicorns, they formed two columns on either side of the children and the refugees. With Jevon in the lead, they all slowly moved forward, with Eddie and Frankie next to Walker, who was leading Lightning.

"For goodness sake, Walker," said Eddie, "get up on your unicorn. What's the point of having one if you don't ride it? It's not a pet, you know."

"I would kind of feel uncomfortable doing that," Walker told him. "We were all in this together, and I don't want it to look like I'm trying to take all the credit myself."

"Well, that depends on whether there is credit to be had," said Eddie. "I'm not sure that Lady Lumina's going to be quite as overjoyed about what we did as Lord Jevon is. We disobeyed her orders, after all. And in my experience she's not one to forgive and forget easily."

"He's got a point," Frankie agreed. "Just because we saved the Kingdom doesn't mean we're the flavor of the month in her mind."

As it happened, she couldn't have been more wrong. By the time they approached the gates they could see flags waving from the ramparts, and flocks of citizens gathered. The news of their victory had spread quickly as soon as the knights accompanying the children of Litherium told everyone what had happened. When the three friends were within earshot, they could hear cheering that got louder and louder the closer they came. When they were a short distance from the walls, the knights raced their unicorns forward and lined up on either side of the gates, tilting their lances to make a tunnel of shining metal beneath which the children would pass.

The huge gates slowly opened to reveal a party of the Kingdom's highest dignitaries waiting to welcome them home. It was, of course, headed by Lumina, and behind her was gathered every member of the Lightkeepers, and behind them were more riders holding banners displaying the Kingdom's symbol.

Frankie, as always, loved being the center of attention, and Eddie looked more like a prince than ever before. He seemed to have grown, both in height and dignity. His long copper-colored hair streamed out behind him, and his bright green eyes flashed, taking in every detail of the scene. As they came through the gates Walker noticed a strange, reddish mark on Eddie's cheekbone.

"What happened to your face?" he asked.

"I don't know," Eddie replied. "What can you see?"

"There's a sort of red mark there."

Eddie rubbed the place that Walker had noticed.

"Yeah," he said, "it's a bit sore. I think it must be where the darkning bolt hit me. It's probably just a bruise."

Frankie saw what Walker was talking about and she ran in front of Eddie, stopping him and the entire column.

"Whoa!" she cried. "That's no bruise. Look where it is, and look what it's doing. That, prince boy, is the mark!"

And sure enough, as they stood and watched it the "bruise" began to transform itself from a red blotch to the identical sun-shaped symbol that Walker carried on his own cheek.

"Is she right?" Eddie asked Walker, his voice quavering with excitement.

"She is," Walker assured him in astonishment. "You have the mark."

Eddie put out his hand and grabbed hold of Walker's shoulder as if he needed support or he would fall to the ground.

"Do you realize what this means?" he asked in a quiet voice. "It means the end of wandering. It means I can grow to be a man after all these years."

"It means, Your Highness, that you are home; you are where you belong."

Lumina had approached them and she, too, had seen the emblem of the Kingdom that was now clearly visible on Eddie's face.

"Your restoration to the rank of Chosen One is a just reward for the courage you and your friends showed when you went into Diabolonia," she continued. "Sometimes we elders have to be taught by children, and everything you did has shown me that it is not enough just to love peace; sometimes you must take strong actions to preserve it. You took those actions and we are proud of you."

There was a roar of cheering from the crowd. Frankie leaned over to Walker and whispered in his ear.

"Does that mean we're off the hook?"

He grinned at her.

"I think it does," he said, "but I also think you can get back on really easily."

"Tell me about it," Frankie muttered. "I've spent most of my life on the hook one way or another."

Lumina took Walker and Eddie by the hand, and she turned to Frankie.

"Follow us, child. I only have two hands and these I must reserve for the Chosen Ones, but you are none the less deserving."

Then she led all three toward one of the statues of ancient kings that flanked the road leading to the gates. The sculpture had been placed on a stone platform with steps leading up to it, and these they mounted, raising them up above the heads of the crowd, which Lumina now addressed.

"Citizens of Nebula," she began. "Today we start a new chapter in the history of this happy realm, for never before have we been blessed with the presence of two Chosen Ones. Between them they have saved the King-dom and rescued the citizens of a Sister City from the bondage of the Black Count. We also owe much to a young woman from the Outerworld who put herself at high risk in the defense of our Kingdom, and for this I say we must recognize her as the lady she surely is. From now on all will address her as 'my lady' and grant her all the honors of her high status in this realm."

Waves of renewed cheering washed over them.

"Lady Frankie," said Frankie. "Cool."

"Oh dear, oh dear, oh dear," sighed Fussingham. "I must remember to write that down in the Book of the Kingdom."

As the cheering died down Walker took his hand from Lumina's and turned to face both her and Eddie. He bowed and addressed them formally.

"Lady Lumina, Your Royal Highness. Until Prince Edward found me I didn't know I was a Chosen One. I'm glad he brought me to the Kingdom, because I love it here and I'm really happy that we beat the Warriors. But I never wanted to be special, or a leader, or anything like that. That's why I didn't want to be king, even though King Leukos wanted me to because there wasn't anyone else with the mark. Well, now there is—Prince Edward—and he's my good friend along with Lady Frankie." He turned to Frankie and was surprised to see her blushing when he used her full title.

"Eddie really is the boy who was born to be king," he continued. "It's time he fulfilled his destiny and became the next ruler of Nebula. Whatever my future holds, it's in the Outerworld, but Eddie's is here. This is where he belongs; this is his home."

He turned to his friend, who stood tall and regal, and he knelt in front of him.

"I will give to you my loyalty and friendship forever, and I will call you majesty for as long as I know you."

"Bless me," muttered Fussingham. "More changes. How I hate change."

CHAPTER 24

Eddie's coronation produced much excitement and celebration in the Kingdom. There were parties in the streets, with music and dancing, and everything in Nebula seemed to glow brighter. So much happened in such a short time that it all became a jumble of memories in Walker's head. He remembered walking up the avenue next to Eddie, with Frankie on his other side, then mounting a tall platform with his friends and placing a crown on Eddie's head. He remembered watching spectacular fireworks burst in the ever-dark sky and the parties and dances that went on for several cycles. One night not long after the coronation, he was watching a party in the Palace courtyard when he suddenly realized that Eddie was standing by his side.

"Let's get away from here for a while," the young king whispered in his ear.

As quietly as possible they left the courtyard and went up into the Royal Apartments. The rooms leading to the king's bedroom were empty now; all of the Lightkeepers were celebrating below.

"I need to stand in front of the Source," said Eddie. "We've never been together. Why don't we do it now?"

Walker agreed, and the two friends made their way down the winding passages that led to the Sanctuary. This time it was Eddie who put the mark on his cheek next to the eye that would release the final panel to allow them access. As it slid open they were bathed in the intense light. Eddie took Walker's hand and together they ascended the steps toward the brilliant globe. Like before, Walker lost all sense of time. He had no idea how long they remained there, or why they both decided at the same moment it was time to leave. It was as if the Source itself determined how long they should stay. When the panel in the king's bedroom closed behind them they stood looking at each other.

"You have to go back to the Outerworld, don't you?" Eddie said.

"Yes," Walker replied. "It's where I belong, in the same way that this is where you belong."

"You're right," said Eddie. "It's destiny, I guess. There's some things you just can't avoid, and even if you could, you wouldn't be happy." He paused for a moment. "I'll miss you."

"Me too," Walker agreed. "But you can still come and get me."

"I will," Eddie assured him. "Believe me, I will, especially when things get a bit tricky, as they're bound to."

Walker smiled. "Maybe you could get me when they're going along fine as well."

"Now what would be the point of that?" Eddie said with his wicked grin across his face.

They looked at each other silently, as if they both realized that this moment was a turning point in their friendship, and that nothing would be the same after it.

"I want to be a really good king," Eddie said.

"And you will be," Walker assured him.

"But I have to do it by myself," Eddie continued.

"I know that, too," Walker agreed.

"Yes, well, that's the problem with you," Eddie retorted, smiling at his friend. "You know too much. It's all those books you read."

"Do you know that I haven't read a book for Eons?" said Walker. "You're a bad influence on me."

"Not just me," protested Eddie. "Frankie as well."

"You're probably right," Walker agreed. "There's just one thing I still don't understand."

"And what's that?"

"Why didn't King Leukos use the Ancient Cry of Peril when you were out there with him in Diabolonia?" Walker asked.

"It only works when the Chosen One has no alternative but to cry for help. As long as there's another way it's the Chosen One's duty to fight on," Eddie explained. "Besides, Leukos was a trained soldier. It was second nature for him to fight."

The two boys began to make their way back to the king's bedroom that was Eddie's now. Eddie sat on the bed, took off his crown, and furiously scratched his head.

"You know, that's a fine piece of work, but it itches like crazy."

"Yeah," said Walker, "I kind of miss the fedora."

"Me too," replied Eddie, "only don't tell Lumina."

"You're a bit scared of her, aren't you?" Walker said.

"Me—scared of Lumina? Never! Well, maybe a little bit," Eddie confessed. "She reminds me of the governess I had many Eons ago."

"Well," said Walker, "I suppose I'd better find Frankie and get back to the Outerworld."

"That's right, I keep forgetting King Leukos told you how to return," said Eddie. "You can pop in anytime you like."

"Providing my dad hasn't filled in the hole in the yard," Walker pointed out.

"Actually, you don't need the hole," Eddie assured him. "It's just a way of focusing your energy. Besides, you've got the unicorn now."

"What do you mean?" asked Walker.

"She can take you back and forth easy as anything," Eddie told him. "All you have to do is sit on her and think of where you're going."

"A unicorn can take you to the Outerworld?" asked Walker in amazement.

"A Silverstreak can," Eddie replied. "They can go everywhere."

Just then the drapes that separated the bedroom from the antechamber opened and Jevon peered in.

"The Lightkeepers are assembled, Your Majesty," he said.

"I'll be right there, Lord Jevon," said Eddie.

"Very well, Your Majesty," said Jevon, and backed away, allowing the curtains to fall back into place.

"Did you see my decree?" Eddie asked Walker.

"The one about Jevon becoming Master of the Royal Household?"

"Yes," said Eddie, "and also Lord Protector of the Realm. I've also decided I'm going to forgive Astrodor. After all, he was only following orders, and it's good to have a few people who do. You and I don't seem to be too good at it. I'm going to make him a Knight Apprentice. If he does well, he'll become a Lightkeeper, and we know he'll do well. He so wants to be one."

"You're right—he does," Walker agreed. "Okay, you're busy with all those meetings with the Lightkeepers and stuff. We'd better be going."

"Oh, spare me the meetings," Eddie growled. "If I'd have known being king involved so many of them I'd have thought twice about taking the job in the first place."

"No, you wouldn't," said Walker. "You love it."

"Well, I suppose you're right," Eddie admitted, "but I also need some action."

"I know. 'Action, my friend, is the secret of success in this life, not book learning.'" Walker quoted him. "That was one of the things you told me when we first met."

"And it's still true," Eddie assured him.

"Maybe," said Walker. "But the action I'm going to take now is to find Frankie and Lightning and get back home."

"Wait," said Eddie. "We can't just let you disappear. We've got to give you a proper send-off. I'm going to postpone this stupid meeting. I am the king, after all."

"Yes." Walker smiled. "You really are."

Shortly after Eddie made this decision, a large crowd gathered along the wide avenue leading to the gates. Jevon, Lumina, Astrodor, and all the Lightkeepers were there along with many hundreds of citizens. Some of the refugees they had rescued were also in the gathering. The energy they got from the Source had so restored them to health that it was difficult to believe they were the same sad individuals who had shuffled into the Kingdom.

Frankie was still dancing when Walker and Eddie found her, and now she and Lightning stood ready to make the return journey to the Outerworld. Walker was just about to give Eddie a hug and jump on his unicorn when a herald blew a loud series of notes on an instrument that looked like a metal cow horn.

"Now hear this!" the herald shouted in her loudest voice. "It is hereby decreed by His Majesty King Edward the Wise that the Chosen One named Walker is made Knight Permanent of the Court of Nebula and Royal Brother to the King. He will be accorded all the rights and entitlements of a Prince of the Realm. Further to this, the Outerworlder Frances Livonia Hayes is named Royal Friend to the King and Privileged Citizen of the Kingdom of Nebula."

Cheering and applause broke out at this announcement.

"He didn't make me a princess?" whispered Frankie to Walker.

"He didn't have to," Walker whispered back. "You already were one."

Frankie stuck out her tongue at him.

When the applause died down Eddie went up to Walker and put his arms on his shoulders.

"You're a good friend," he said, "and wiser than I am for all the many hundreds of your years I've been around. Come back and see us often, and remember that you are a Chosen One, not only here, but in the Outerworld as well."

"I will," Walker promised, and Eddie gave him an enormous bear hug that left him gasping for air. It started a flurry of hugging, and even Lumina joined in. Frankie threw her arms around Eddie's neck.

"Well, old king thing," she said, "don't forget to have fun while you're doing all this ruling stuff, because you do take yourself a bit too seriously at times."

"I suppose," Eddie said, "that there's no chance of you being deferential in my royal presence."

"None whatsoever," she agreed.

And so they mounted Lightning.

"How on earth am I going to explain to my parents that I'm the proud owner of a unicorn?" Walker asked Eddie.

"Don't worry," Eddie told him. "When you get back to the Outerworld she'll turn into a horse. Just tell them you're looking after it for a friend or something. Now get out of here."

Eddie gently slapped Lightning on her rear and she began to gallop toward the gates. Just when it appeared she would crash into them, Lightning unfolded her wings and began to soar up into the air. She circled around the Kingdom so that Walker and Frankie could see the people looking up and waving. Then she spiraled higher and higher and Nebula got smaller and smaller until it looked like a sparkling jewel on a black velvet cushion.

"Okay, Chosen One," Frankie said as she clung tightly to his waist, "it's time to start concentrating on where we want to land, and try not to hit the barn this time."

And with that, they disappeared into the darkness that would bring them home.